Dagger's Hope:
The Alliance Book 3

By S.E. Smith

Acknowledgments

I would like to thank my husband Steve for believing in me and being proud enough of me to give me the courage to follow my dream. I would also like to give a special thank you to my sister and best friend, Linda, who not only encouraged me to write, but who also read the manuscript. Also to my other friends who believe in me: Julie, Jackie, Lisa, Sally, Elizabeth (Beth) and Narelle. The girls that keep me going!
—S.E. Smith

Montana Publishing
Science Fiction Romance
Dagger's Hope: The Alliance Book 3
Copyright © 2015 by S.E. Smith
First E-Book Published March 2015
Cover Design by Melody Simmons

Summary: Dagger was sold into a fight ring where he's slowly going insane, clinging to a single hope: Jordan.

ISBN: 978-1-942562-50-4 (paperback)
ISBN: 978-1-942562-14-6 (eBook)

Published in the United States by Montana Publishing.

{1. Science Fiction Romance – Fiction. 2. Science Fiction – Fiction. 3. Paranormal – Fiction. 4. Romance – Fiction.}

www.montanapublishinghouse.com

Synopsis

Dagger is a Trivator warrior. He is known for his dark and dangerous edge, making him the perfect warrior for impossible missions. He fears nothing, until he meets a young, delicate human female who wakens his heart. Her gentle touch, soft voice, and her shy sense of humor touch him in a way he never thought could happen. The thought of anything harming something so beautiful and fragile fills him with terror.

Jordan Sampson is slowly adjusting to her new life on a strange planet far away from war-torn Earth. She had been seventeen when she was brought to the Trivator's home world of Rathon along with her older sister, Jesse, and younger sister, Taylor, a couple years earlier. Fear, confusion, and uncertainty of what the future holds threaten to drown her as she tries to fit in. There is only one hope that keeps her going. It is the handsome alien male that stirs something deep inside her and makes her feel whole.

When Dagger is captured during a mission and sold to the illegal Fight Rings, it is only the memory of Jordan that keeps him going. Time blurs as he slowly sinks deeper and deeper into a world of violence and pain until he becomes more animal than Trivator.

Jordan knows Dagger is out there, somewhere. She can feel him in her heart. The heart she gave to him the first time he held her protectively in his arms. When she discovers where he is being held, she refuses to let anything stop her from rescuing him. What Jordan doesn't realize is that she has been

Dagger's hope during his captivity. The one thing that holds the thin thread to his sanity.

The fight to save Dagger takes Jordan on a journey that she hopes they both survive. The star system is a dangerous place for a young human female and a damaged Trivator warrior. Can Jordan reach Dagger in time, and if she does, can she heal his shattered soul?

Contents

Chapter 1

Dagger clung to the top of the cage holding him, his back pressed upward against the cold metal. He had braced his feet in the narrow slats and held onto the thick bars with his left hand as he watched the secondary door slowly open. In his right hand, he held a long chain filled with razor-sharp blades designed to slice through flesh and bone.

He ignored the blood running down his arm, watching disconnectedly as it dripped to the floor of the cage far below him. Holding his body perfectly still, he waited for the massive creature under him to turn. A sense of cold calculation kept his mind sharp, even as his body threatened to weaken from exhaustion.

"Fight, fight, fight, fight!" The crowd chanted, wanting him to drop down.

Dagger tuned out the crowd. He had seen what was about to be released into the cage with him and the other male long before they did. He knew if he was to survive, he had to use every skill he possessed.

As it was, three out of the four men that had been in the cage with him were already dead. The fourth man wouldn't last long from the way he drunkenly staggered away from the door. The man was coated with blood, both from his own wounds and from the blood of the male he had just killed. The beast would attack the moment it caught the scent of him, which was why Dagger had turned and climbed up the woven half-dome bars that formed the cage.

He had killed two of the males that littered the ring. The crowds surrounding the cage had screamed for him to finish the other two men that were locked in a battle of life or death, but he had ignored their demands. He knew that he needed to conserve his strength for what was to come.

Instead, he fell back against the side of the cage and drew deep, calming breaths as his eyes roamed the arena searching for the one responsible for him being there. He knew the male was somewhere in the crowd watching him. Dagger could feel the male's gloating gaze on him, just as he did every time he fought.

His eyes scanned over the packed arena. For a moment, he paused on the Drethulan sitting in the box seat high above the crowds. While Jolin Talja owned and operated the fight ring called *The Hole* now, he was second on Dagger's list for termination.

No, he was searching for the one who thought he 'owned' him; the one that lent him to the owners of the illegal underground groups that enjoyed the profit of watching men and women like Dagger fight for survival. Dagger was an enigma. He had survived longer than any of the other fighters, so far, and was the most profitable one to date for both his 'owner' and those who bet on him to win.

His eyes froze on the third row up as a familiar set of beady black eyes stared intently back at him. For a moment, everything around Dagger narrowed to the one figure leisurely sitting back in the reserved box in the stands. Their eyes locked in a silent battle of will; one in triumph, the other in promise.

The pale white complexion of the male stood out among the other colorful spectators in the stands. He didn't try to hide his face in an effort to remain anonymous. He knew that Dagger would search him out and he wanted to be found. A deep hatred burned bitterly inside Dagger, threatening to boil over until he thought he would explode.

He stared back at Cordus Kelman. The billionaire mercenary's bald head shone brightly under the lights of the arena. He was on the most wanted list in numerous star systems. The bastard was smart enough to stay on the outskirts of the Alliance's boundaries, not quite out of it, but not quite in it either.

Kelman stayed in the space that was considered primitive and dangerous to any who entered. It was a lawless area that no star system wanted to deal with because they knew that as long as the area existed, then those that inhabited it would stay out of their own regions. That had been true until Kelman attacked the planet where Hunter, Dagger, and several other Trivator forces were trying to regain control. The attack had turned out to be a trap.

Kelman had been the mastermind behind the staged battle that led to his capture. He didn't know what happened to his partner, Edge. Dagger had been knocked unconscious when their transport had crashed. That had been over two years ago. Since then, Kelman had attended every fight Dagger had been forced to participate in. The mercenary watched him night after night, gloating at the rage and creeping insanity that was slowly taking over Dagger's mind.

Dagger's eyes broke contact when he heard the hoarse scream of the last male as the beast under him turned. The male hung by a leg for a brief moment before he disappeared down the creature's throat. The sickening sound of bones being crushed was muted by the shrieks of the audience.

Dagger waited, the arm holding him locked at the elbow, in an effort to keep his body still as the beast turned in a circle, sniffing the air. The Gartaian was a mammoth gray creature that lived in the swampy areas of the planet Kepler-10. He had only seen images of them in some of the training videos he had watched during his downtime on board the different warships over the years.

The creature stood almost four meters high and weighed in at over ten thousand kilograms. A series of three tusks in varying sizes protruded from each side of its mouth, allowing it to uproot trees and other debris in its constant search for food, as well as provide protection for it. It was genetically enabled to eat and digest anything. The Gartaian's tongue could reach out almost two meters, allowing it to drag its prey into its wide mouth. The teeth were thick and flat and were designed for crushing whatever it found before it swallowed the remains of its prey. Being crushed and eaten was not on Dagger's list of ways to die.

The Gartaian had one weakness that Dagger knew of, it was virtually blind. It depended almost solely on its sense of smell. The one advantage Dagger had, was that the arena was coated in the blood of the dead men and covered his own scent.

He waited patiently until the beast turned in a semicircle, presenting its thick, gray back to him. Pushing off the bars with his feet, he released his grip and fell onto the creature's back. The long, blade-filled chain in his hand swung around and under the beast's chin. He bent forward, grabbing the end of it with the tips of his fingers as it swung back up on the other side of the creature's neck.

Dagger tightened his grip on each end, knowing that if he lost the advantage he had, that it would all be over. Leaning back, the muscles in his arms strained as he pulled the razor sharp blades against the beast's thick flesh. The loud, furious roar from it shook the arena.

Locking his knees behind the creature's neck and pressing his heels into its massive shoulders, he began working his hands back and forth in a sawing motion. He was almost unseated when the beast swung around and slammed its body into the metal cage. The only thing saving him from being crushed between the huge body and the metal cage was that his left leg was pressed along the inside curve of its shoulder, protecting it.

The force of the blow was enough to bend the bars. The spectators standing near the cage jerked back, some screaming and falling as others pushed to get away from the long tongue snaking out. One female that had fallen wasn't fast enough. Her loud, piercing scream filled the chaotic stands when the tongue slipped through the bars and wound around her ankle. Those surrounding her pushed to get away instead of helping her as the Gartaian pulled her forward.

The loud screams from the female suddenly died when her leg snapped and was ripped away as the Gartaian tried to pull her through the narrow slits. Dagger ignored everything, but his continued assault on the beast's throat. He felt when the thick flesh gave way under the sharp blades and the softer flesh under the skin was opened to him.

The Gartaian stumbled as he sliced through the main artery in its neck. A wave of black blood poured from the pulsing wound, coating the floor of the arena in a thick, putrid stench as it flowed through the bars. Keeping a constant pressure, he waited until its front legs gave out on it and it began to collapse before he released the tip of the blade and swung it back around in a high arc.

The end of the deadly whip wrapped around the bar at the top of the cage. Dagger released his grip as the beast fell from under him, holding on to the end of the whip with both hands. The spectators' cries and screams had turned to a stunned silence as the Gartaian drew in a last shuddering breath before its tongue rolled out of its mouth and its eyes glazed over in death.

Dagger could feel the hundreds of eyes on him as he hung from the center of the cage, his body slowly rotating. His own eyes stared back in rage as he glared back at them. It was only when his eyes swept over a lone figure, standing off to one side at the very top of the arena, that the fury dissolved.

He would have missed the slender, cloaked figure if he hadn't been so high. He watched as pale hands reached up and slid the hood of the cloak back to reveal the face hidden in its shadow. For just a moment, no more than half of a second, his eyes locked with a pair of haunted hazel eyes.

Dagger's throat worked up and down as he watched the figure quickly replace the hood and step back into the dark recess as another figure approached. His arms trembled as the last of his strength drained from him. Glancing down, he released his grip on the whip and dropped down onto the side of the dead Gartaian. He knelt on one knee and breathed deeply as confusion flooded his mind.

The loud applause from the spectators washed over him, pulsing through his exhausted mind. He rose up on the beast he had landed on, trying to see over the standing crowd. A loud hiss of rage escaped him when he felt the loop of the long poles around his wrists as the guards rushed to contain him. He fought briefly, trying desperately to see over the heads of the cheering crowd, but it was useless. Sliding off the back of the Gartaian, Dagger stiffened his shoulders as Kelman stepped into the entrance gate, slowly clapping his hands.

"Well done, Trivator," Kelman mockingly chuckled. "I earned a year's supply of Vaspian liquor off of this fight."

Dagger jerked forward, dragging the guards on each side of him. Kelman took a step back, a narrow, thoughtful look on his face. Three more guards surged around Kelman. Dagger staggered when one of them hit him in the chest with a power rod. He trembled for a moment before his legs gave out as the man hit him again with another powerful shock.

"I... will... kill you," Dagger hissed out as his head fell forward.

His shoulders burned as the guards holding him, dragged him out of the arena and back down to the cells three floors below the fight ring. Nausea and exhaustion competed with the pain from the deep cut on his shoulder and back. The pain and exhaustion he could handle. It was the nausea that was almost his undoing. Nausea that his fractured mind would be so desperate to see Jordan Sampson one last time that it would make him think she would be in such a place as *The Hole*.

"Never," he whispered in a voice hoarse with disuse.

He blinked several times, trying to clear his vision in the dim lighting. The guards had dropped his body on the cold, hard stone floor. Two of them stood over him, holding his wrists to the floor as two more reattached the chains to the cuffs on his wrists and ankles.

Once that was done, the healer stepped into the cell. Kelman always sent the healer in after a fight to take care of his wounds. The mercenary wanted Dagger ready for the next competition.

His eyes closed as the healer doctored the wound on his arm and shoulder. The old male muttered nonsense under his breath before he slapped an injector to Dagger's neck and depressed the trigger.

Dagger didn't bother opening his eyes as the old man rose unsteadily back to his feet. A minute later, silence filled the long corridor. He was the only prisoner on this level. They had separated him from the others shortly after he arrived when he had incited several of the other fighters into attacking the guards.

Rolling over onto his back, he gazed up at the ceiling. He could feel the medicine coursing through his system, numbing the pain and pulling him toward sleep. Something told him that the old healer had defied orders when he gave him the injection.

For a moment, Dagger fought to keep his eyes open, but exhaustion pulled at him. His mind wandered aimlessly before a beautiful, pale face rose to push everything else away. Jordan. It was her face that he saw in the quiet solitude of his cell between fights.

He was afraid he was finally losing his hold on sanity. He could have sworn he saw her, but he knew that was impossible. Regret and loneliness sent a chill through his body. Releasing the tight control he kept over his mind, he opened his memories, hoping they would warm him for the few hours he would be given until the next fight.

"Please," he whispered in a soft, rusty voice. "Please keep her safe."

He gave up on trying to stay awake. Instead, he thought back to the first time he saw Jordan Sampson. Regret burned through him that he wouldn't be able to keep the promise he gave to her the last time he saw her. It was that promise and the one and only time he had kissed her that gave him hope and the determination to fight until his dying breath.

An unfamiliar burning in his eyes caused them to water. He would never admit the tear that squeezed past his tightly closed eyelids. Because to admit it, would be to admit that he had given up all hope of ever seeing her again.

Chapter 2

Two and a half years before - Earth:

"The female went this way," Dagger said, rising from where he had been kneeling beside a burnt out human transport. They were in a narrow alley several blocks from the warehouse where Hunter had been held prisoner. They were trying to find the human female that had released Hunter from where he was being held captive. "Are you sure this isn't another trap, Hunter?"

"This is no trap," Hunter replied in a clipped tone, gazing around in frustration. "I have to find her... tonight."

Dagger shrugged and watched as another shadowy figure stepped up and laid his hand on Hunter's shoulder. Out of the three of them, Saber was the most easy-going and optimistic. Dagger turned away so he could continue following the trail of blood the human female left behind.

Personally, he thought his friend was making a huge mistake trying to locate her. So far, he wasn't that impressed with most of the humans he had met over the last four years. Of course, the ones they encountered were usually the ones trying to kill him, Saber, and Hunter.

There were some good ones, too, he had to admit. He had respect for the difficult task the human military was having trying to control their people. Still, he thought it better to keep a distance from the humans as much as possible, especially with their tour here almost completed.

"We'll find her," Saber promised before turning to look up at the dark sky with a scowl. "Why did we have to get stuck in a region where it pisses down on us all the time?"

A gruff chuckle escaped Dagger. "Because you were the one who decided it would be fun to try to introduce Jag to the human nurse that wanted to thread your skin together when you got cut during our mission six months ago, Saber. You should have known better than to piss off your commanding officer," he retorted. "I've found more blood this way. We'd better find your missing warrior soon while we still have the scent of her blood to follow, Hunter, or we'll be doing it the hard way. I don't relish trying to look in every hole that she could hide in."

"How was I supposed to know that she was vicious? She was a healer! Aren't all healers supposed to be gentle?" Saber grumbled and shook his head, slinging water droplets everywhere. "I still don't think it warranted being sent here. I heard that a place called Hawaii was nice."

"Well, you won't get to find out," Dagger said, glancing down to see if he could find the faint trail again. "Personally, I can't wait to get off this rock. Our time is almost up here. I'm ready for a change."

"What are you going to do?" Hunter asked distractedly. He paused and frowned when he saw the faint outline of a bloody palm print on the side of the brick building. Touching it, he raised his fingers to his nose. "This is hers."

Dagger shrugged. He didn't know what he would do when his tour expired in a few months. He might enlist into the same division his older brother Trig was assigned to or go off on his own. He didn't have much to tie him to Rathon. He had a home there, but hadn't spent more than a dozen nights in it in over ten years.

Hunter was scheduled to return to his duties back on Rathon. Maybe Saber would join as well. After all, the three of them had made a great team over the last ten years. With Hunter gone and their required duty completed, he and Saber could do some exploring. There was a new star system that had joined the Alliance and he wouldn't mind seeing what it was like.

Hell, it would even be nice to return home for some real female company. It had been four years since he'd had a chance to be with a female that could match him in the bedroom. The human females were pleasant, but the two he spent any time with had done little to heat his blood. He was beginning to think that would never happen.

"Probably join up with Trig," Dagger replied with a shrug, frowning when he couldn't find any more tracks. "Saber, do you see anything?"

"No, her tracks have disappeared again," Saber bit out in frustration, walking in a slow circle before stopping to glance around the rubble of buildings littering the area. "She must have doubled back again. She's good at doing that."

"No," Hunter murmured, looking at the pile of concrete lying at a forty-five degree angle across the road from them. "She is here. I can feel it in my gut."

"Yeah, but where is here?" Dagger asked, running his hand through his long white hair. "There is a mountain of rubble that she could be hiding in."

He watched as Hunter walked ahead of him, his eyes focused on the ground. He crossed the road and knelt, looking at something on the ground. Dagger followed behind him, noticing the slight heel indent in the dirt as well when he got closer.

He almost called out a warning when Hunter suddenly disappeared down a narrow opening between two large slabs. When Hunter didn't reappear, he glanced at Saber and shrugged. Stepping up to the dark recess, he saw that it actually slid downward. He could barely make out Hunter's figure in the darkness below.

Ducking his head, he stepped onto the thick slab of concrete and slid down until he was standing next to his friend. A moment later, Saber was standing next to him. He shook his head in amazement. In the confines of the enclosed area, he could smell the blood of the female mixed with additional scents. He had to admit, Hunter's female was smart.

He nodded when Hunter held up his hand before signaling them that there were more humans in the area. He could hear a soft murmur of voices and caught the faint glow and the scent of a fire. Moving silently, he flanked Hunter's left side as they moved toward the group.

* * *

The area was littered with trapped vehicles. Some of the vehicles were crushed from where parts of the building had collapsed, while others remained intact, trapped in what was now an underground tomb. They moved through the dark area with ease, heading for the faint flicker of light. Stepping around a thick concrete support, all three of them froze for a moment as they took in the heart-wrenching scene in front of them.

Nestled in the corner between the thick walls of the underground parking garage and a dark blue transport on the other side were two human females. They both appeared to be very young. One sat beside the makeshift fire pit constructed of building debris while the other lay on the hard ground. What was heart-wrenching was the realization that this cold, dark and stark area was their home.

Dagger's eyes swept over the first figure before settling on the second. He drew in a swift breath and stared at the female lying weakly on the makeshift pallet on the cold concrete floor. He had been totally unprepared for the sudden onslaught of emotion that hit him when he saw her pale, heart-shaped face.

She was facing his direction, giving him an unobstructed view of her pain-filled eyes. It felt like he had been struck in the chest. In fact, his hand actually started to rub at the discomfort. He watched the small figure of the other female rise with a steaming cup in her hand. She quickly moved to help her companion who struggled to sit up.

His eyes were arrested by the sheer delicate beauty in the female that was leaning weakly against the other young woman, as if she didn't have the strength to do so on her own. The firelight highlighted her delicate bone structure as she gazed at her companion. In the dim light, he could see dark bruises marring the pale skin of her right cheek when the other woman brushed her hair back from her face. Fury churned inside him, making his eyes glow with a dark, dangerous light.

He watched as she turned to smother her cough. It was obvious that it left her even weaker. A sick feeling washed over him as he wondered if this was the female Hunter was searching for. He hoped not.

The thought of his friend claiming the fragile human made him almost double over as another wave of emotion hit him... jealousy. The strange primitive instinct to protect and care for the female gripped him tightly in its grasp as she struggled to keep from sinking back down to the pallet. It was obvious that she was both ill and hurt.

Dagger glanced at Hunter to see his reaction to the scene in front of him. He almost fell to his knees in relief when his friend glanced at him with a dark frown and shook his head. He nodded when Hunter raised his hand and held up two fingers before raising a third one.

Dagger breathed a sigh of relief. There were three females. Three! Neither one of the two was the one Hunter was searching for. Dagger turned his attention back to the two by the fire. His eyes narrowed as he watched the younger one help his female to sit up again when she started to slide back down.

Mine, he thought in stunned disbelief. *My female.*

Dagger barely registered the softly spoken words as the two women talked. His eyes were glued to the pale face, trembling hands and fragile form as she moaned and closed her eyes in pain. It took every ounce of discipline he had to remain still. His body shook as he fought to remain in position. He couldn't compromise the mission. He repeated that over and over as he clenched his fists.

"Are you still hurting a lot, Jordan?" The young female asked with concern. "Maybe Jesse found some medicine for you when she was out tonight. I think your fever isn't as bad as it was earlier."

"I'm... I'm okay, Taylor," Jordan whispered in a low, husky voice. "Where is Jesse? It shouldn't take her this long."

"She said she had a cut she needed to clean," Taylor replied as she slid her arm around to balance Jordan when she started to slide back down onto the pallet. "She'll be back any minute. You need to eat. This will help you get stronger."

Glazed hazel eyes blinked and a weak smile curved the female named Jordan's lips as the younger girl held the steaming cup up to her mouth. He didn't miss the way her hands trembled as she weakly took the nourishment. His body jerked forward in protest as her softly spoken words ripped through him.

"I don't think I'll ever be strong again," Jordan whispered, dark despair making her words echo with sorrow.

Dagger had to strain to hear Jordan's soft words. When they registered, the unfamiliar wave of alarm and a fierce determination to help her gripped him. He could hear the pain and exhaustion in her response. A cold fury burned in him at the human males that had hurt her. He had no doubt that is what happened as he stared at her face.

"Don't!" Taylor hissed, holding the cup up to Jordan's lips. "We promised each other we would never give up. It is okay to feel down. You deserve it after… well, you deserve it, but don't ever give up, Jordan. We need you. I need you."

"I can do this," Jordan whispered. "You need to eat too."

He watched as the young female called Taylor, reluctantly handed the battered cup of soup to Jordan. He felt his body start forward when the cup shook in her hand. She needed immediate medical attention.

All thought of the mission, the need to find the other female, disappeared from his mind as he watched her. He ignored Hunter as he moved off into the darkness. With a determination born out of confusion and concern, he silently stepped forward.

She will be safe and strong once again, he thought as he stepped into the faint light cast by the fire. *I will make sure that she is.*

* * *

Jordan didn't want to admit to her little sister just how weak she was. There was no way that she would be able to continue if they should have to move again. She was pretty sure that at least one of her ribs had been broken when the man had attacked her the other night in the alley.

Bitter tears glittered in her eyes. She had made a stupid mistake. She should have realized that Jesse wasn't behind her. If she had waited…

No, she thought in resignation. *If I had waited, both Jesse and I would have been attacked and Taylor would have been alone.*

Jordan tried to still the trembling in her hands. She didn't think she would ever feel warm or full or safe again. She felt… dirty, both inside and out. A small part of her wanted to just give up. She felt like if she could just lie down and close her eyes, she could just let go and never wake up again.

Her eyes flickered to Taylor. If it wasn't for her older sister, Jesse, and Taylor, she would. She was tired of running and of being scared and of always being hungry and exhausted.

She was… Her eyes widened when a black, menacing shadow moved out of the darkness. Golden yellow eyes glowed in the dim light cast by their small fire. In the back of her mind, she registered that there were two separate shapes moving toward them, but her eyes were locked with the pair staring at her.

Long white hair hung down past the man's shoulders. He was dressed all in black, making it even more difficult to see him. She knew immediately that he wasn't human. He was too confident, too muscular, and even more dangerous than the ones they had encountered on the streets over the last few years.

No, this was a killing machine, a Trivator warrior, an… alien. Her hand began to shake uncontrollably, spilling some of the precious liquid in it onto the blanket wrapped around her legs. Her eyes grew wider as he continued to approach them, a low growl escaped him, causing her to begin to pant in distress.

"What's wrong?" Taylor asked, turning around.

"Run," Jordan forced out, never taking her eyes off of the men walking toward them. "Find Jesse and run, Taylor. Now!"

A low cry escaped Taylor. Jordan dropped the cup of soup and tried to rise in an effort to give Taylor time to escape. She paled and almost fainted at the pain running through her at the movement. Opening her mouth, she was about to order Taylor to run again when her little sister erupted into a flurry of rage.

The years of playing softball helped when Taylor grabbed several pieces of the concrete they were using to bank the fire and threw them. Low curses escaped one of the huge men when a piece caught him in the stomach. Jordan tried to push off the ground again, only to fall back onto the pallet with a loud cry of pain.

The sound distracted Taylor, giving the male she was hitting a chance to rush her. Her loud curses filled the underground garage when he wrapped his arms around her and lifted her off her feet. That didn't stop Taylor. She wildly kicked out and slammed her head back against the man's chin.

"Ouch! You little *shrewta*," the man growled. "Stop before you get hurt!"

"I'm not the one going to be hurting," Taylor promised as she kicked her heel into his shin again. "Let me go! I'm going to tear you apart! I'm going to barbeque your remains and feed them to the wild dogs. I'm going to…"

"Enough," the male holding her grunted when she snapped her teeth at him. "You are a bloodthirsty creature."

"Let her go," Jordan pleaded, lying on the pallet violently shivering. "Please, she is just a child. Please don't hurt her."

"She is no child," the man replied with a hiss. "She is a vicious creature with sharp teeth! That hurts! Let go of my arm. I will feed you real food."

Jordan couldn't understand what Taylor was saying. She had her teeth buried in the man's arm and was growling like the old dog they used to have. She started when she felt a hand on her shoulder. Turning her head, she released a low squeak of fright before crying out again when she tried to move away. Her eyes filled with tears of pain and she moaned as she wrapped her arm protectively around her ribs.

"Please," she begged hoarsely, gripping the hand that moved to touch her bruised cheek. "Please, don't hurt her."

The face gazing down at her, the one that looked so fierce and menacing just moments before, softened.

The dark yellow-gold eyes still glowed, but instead of burning fury, they held concern. Unable to hold her head up any longer, she let her head fall back to the backpack that she was using as a pillow.

"Relax, little warrior," he whispered, glancing at where his friend was still trying to get a firm grip on the other female. A slight smile curved the corner of his lips when Saber released another loud curse. "I think it is my friend who may need to be rescued."

Jordan's eyes flickered to where Taylor had slipped out of the man's hold and was now on his back with her arms wrapped around his neck and her legs around his waist. She would have been more worried if not for the look of exasperation on the man's face as he twirled around in a circle trying to get his hands on her little sister again.

Turning her head back to the man staring down at her, she bit her lip. A shiver shook her as the cold, pain, and reaction started to set in. Her eyelids fluttered closed for a moment only to pop back open when she felt a warm, rough palm against her bruised cheek.

"Who did this to you?" The man demanded in a low voice.

Fear, despair, and shame filled her and she closed her eyes again. Suddenly, everything was too much, the pain and the feeling of being powerless to protect Taylor and Jesse hit her hard. Her body and mind were shutting down on her. Between the beating, the lack of food, and her inability to help protect those she loved, she felt more of a hindrance than ever.

"Just don't... hurt them," she whispered, turning her face into his warmth as the shivers from the cold and her fever began to uncontrollably shake her body.

"Saber," Dagger growled in impatience. "This female needs immediate medical assistance."

"So do I!" Saber snapped back before he winced as the teeth that had been gnawing on his arm a few minutes before now attached to his ear. "Son of a... Will you stop?! You've drawn blood again. We are trying to help you!"

The teeth attached to Saber's ear and the hands around his neck disappeared as if the piranha on his back suddenly vanished into thin air. Turning, he glared at the tiny female's back as she darted around the fire and fell to her knees next to the one lying on the pallet.

"Jordan," Taylor cried out when Jordan didn't respond. The hint of fear thickening it. "Jordan, oh god. You have to help her."

"We need to leave," another deep voice said. "This one is injured and needs medical attention as well."

Dagger nodded when he smelled the blood from the limp figure in Hunter's arms. He looked up into the dark eyes of the small female that had attacked Saber. She gazed back at him in fear, but there was something else in her gaze as well. A touch of hope and a silent plea for help.

"We will get medical assistance for your companions," he promised.

"Sisters," Taylor whispered, rising to her feet and looking back and forth between Jesse and Jordan.

"They are my sisters, my family, the only ones I have left since Dad was killed."

"Saber, call a retrieval transport," Hunter ordered with a sharp look at his friend. "We will return with them to the compound."

Dagger noticed that Saber cast a wary look at Taylor and nodded. He grinned when he saw Saber rub his throbbing ear before he touched the comlink at his collar and muttered into it in their native language. Dagger's eyes were drawn to the half dozen teeth marks on Saber's arm. His friend was right, the young human was a vicious little thing.

..*

Dagger jerked awake when he heard the sound of footsteps approach. Rolling onto his stomach, a low feral growl escaped him as he rose to his feet. His hands wrapped around the chains at his wrists, twisting them to test their strength. They had replaced them while he was in the cage.

"I hope you are rested," one of the guards said, stepping up to the door of Dagger's prison cell. "Eat! You will need every bit of it. You are back in the cage in two hours. I have a lot of money on you to win."

The guard slid the paper-thin tray of food under the door of the cell before hastily jerking back when Dagger stepped forward, straining to break free. He ignored the food. Instead, he focused on the guard's face. He was going to kill every single one of them.

"Eat," the guard ordered before turning.

Dagger waited until the door at the far end of the corridor closed before he bent and picked up several pieces of fruit and the thin slab of barely cooked meat. Drawing back into the shadows in the corner of the cell, he squatted down and bit viciously into the meat. He slowly chewed it before swallowing it. Picking up the dark red fruit, he bit into the soft fruit and drank deeply of the vitamin rich liquid inside it.

Staring up at the surveillance camera, he thought moodily of Kelman and the others. Kelman couldn't see him in the shadows. It was the only place that he could be in the cell without eyes on him. He hated it. Bending his head, he closed his eyes and tried to bring back the image of Jordan's face in his mind, but it was like the shadows that surrounded him, dark and fuzzy.

Is she even real? He wondered as he finished the small meal. *Maybe she is nothing more than a dream.*

Chapter 3

Jordan bowed her head and slipped through the upper door high above the fighting arena, a shadow among the other spectators. She would wait outside for Trig to find her. There was one more event tonight.

Fear and hope gripped her as she hurried down the back staircase. She had stolen one of the worker's badges as he was leaving through the dirty kitchen area. It had helped that the creature had been drunk and didn't feel her fingers as they slipped the badge from his waist when she bumped into him in the side alley behind the narrow buildings.

She had used the badge to access the back entrance. Slipping inside, she had made her way to the ticket booth using the map she had on the small tablet in her hand before it opened. It hadn't taken long for her to hack into their computer system. It was antiquated compared to the Trivator systems. She had wasted no time printing out two tickets to the night's fights.

Keeping the hood of the cloak over her head, she had grabbed the trash and a broom that was in the corner as the door behind her opened. She softly muttered her apology for her lateness in cleaning the room to the fat, wart-covered female that entered the ticket area. The creature had scowled at her, but didn't question Jordan when she held up the badge.

Jordan was shaking from the close call, but even more determined than ever that she had made the right decision. She knew Trig, Dagger's older brother, would be furious about her disappearing on him.

He had kept insisting that she stay locked in the small room he had rented while he searched for Dagger after they had witnessed the brutal slaying of the owner of *The Hole* almost a week ago. She had spent the time searching any records for Dagger or a Trivator warrior on the Spaceport. A flag had risen when the new owner of *The Hole*, a Dreluthan, began promoting that he had a fighter unlike any other. He boasted he had a Trivator warrior that would fight at the establishment against creatures large and small. Each show that week had immediately sold out.

Trig had returned, frustrated that not even the ticket brokers could get any passes to the events. The three that had tried to forge tickets had been brutally killed and left on display in front of *The Hole* as an example of what would happen if any illegal tickets were made.

Trig had explained the Dreluthans were interested in one thing and one thing only, making credits. He wasn't the only one frustrated, so was Jordan. She had waited until he had gone into the bathroom before she disappeared. It was the only way she could. She discovered the first day that he had locked her inside. But, as long as he was there, she would be able to escape.

Jordan set the broom down at the door leading out of the side of the building. She passed at least eight guards on her way out of the building. She discovered that as long as she held up the badge she had stolen in one gloved-covered hand, no one stopped her. Holding the trash in her other hand, she slipped out of the door in the pretense of disposing of it. She quickly tossed the garbage into the compactor outside and walked to the end of the alley. She hoped that Trig wouldn't take too long figuring out where she had gone.

It took almost an hour for him to finally appear. Jordan glanced nervously at the long line of creatures waiting to get inside. Moving out of the shadows, she stepped into Trig's path when he made to move around her.

"Trig," she murmured in a low voice. "It's me."

She glanced up at his face, noting how it turned from a menacing scowl, to surprise, before it turned to fury. She bit her lip when his fingers wrapped around her arm in a bruising grip. He turned her quickly and pulled her into the narrow alley that she had used earlier.

"I ought to whip your ass," Trig growled in a low, furious voice. "I'm taking you back to Rathon. I swore to Hunter I would keep you safe. I can't believe you would go off on your own! Do you have any idea of what could happen to you?"

Jordan winced when his hand unconsciously tightened on her arm. "I found him," she whispered. "I found Dagger."

Trig's mouth snapped shut and he released her arm. Staring broodingly down into her wide, pleading hazel eyes, he bit out another low curse. He should have known better than to agree to take her with him on this mission.

Not that I had much choice, he thought ruefully as he gazed down into her haunted eyes. *She would have kept her promise of finding another way here.*

Running his hands through his hair, he released a long breath. This human female had been a pain in his ass ever since she unexpectedly showed up at Dagger's house the night after he arrived. He later discovered she had been tracking his whereabouts through Hunter's computer system.

His mind flickered back to that night almost a month ago when he returned to Rathon after losing Dagger's trail. He planned to spend the night at Dagger's place before meeting up with Hunter to go over the little information he had found. He had not been expecting a surprise intruder in the middle of the night or their rapid departure.

* * *

Rathon: One month before.

Jordan slipped the tablet she used into the black bag and looked around her bedroom one last time. The note that she had written for Jesse rested against the pillow on her neatly made bed. She adjusted the black cap she was wearing over her sun-streaked brown hair and walked over to the door leading out to the back garden. She would have to be careful not to trip the security grid around Hunter and Jesse's home.

She glanced at the small wrist-size screen attached to her arm. She could control the home security system software she had downloaded on her tablet using it. Closing the door to her bedroom, she silently crossed the covered porch area and moved down the steps.

Once she had reached the side gate, she glanced over her shoulder one last time before she pressed the remote. Counting under her breath, she waited impatiently for the light at the gate to change colors, indicating that it had disengaged. She would have ten seconds from the time the gate unlocked to get through it and close it again before the alarm sounded.

The second the light changed, she opened the first gate and stepped through. She quickly closed it behind her and moved to the second gate which protected the property from the large creatures that moved through the forests. Slipping through it, she closed the gate and watched as the light turned from green to red again.

The sounds of the night echoed around her. It reminded her a little of what it had sounded like up at the cabin her dad had owned in Wenatchee, Washington. She jumped when she heard a loud crash followed by a snarl.

Well, almost, she thought as she hurried down the softly lit path.

Once she was far enough from the house, she pulled her tablet up and sent in a request for a transport pick up. There weren't a lot of houses along the area where Jesse and Hunter lived and because she didn't want to take a chance of Hunter being woken up, she had sent the request to pick her up outside the small park a mile from the house. If she ran, she could be there by the time the unmanned transport arrived.

Jordan secured the black backpack containing a couple of changes of clothes, food, water, a medical scanner, an emergency medical kit, and her tablet on to her back. Breaking into an easy jog, she breathed in and out evenly as she kept a steady pace. A startled cry escaped her a quarter mile from her destination when a huge, dark shape burst out of the forest.

"Oh shit!" Jordan hissed when she realized that one of the bear-like creatures that lived in the forest had caught scent of her.

She weaved, twisting and almost fell when it charged at her. Pulling the small laser pistol she had taken from Hunter's office out of the waistband of her pants, she pointed it at the creature with shaking hands. Standing still with her feet apart like her dad had shown her and Jesse, she waited as it suddenly stopped and rose up on its hind legs.

"Oh, double shit," she whispered as her eyes rose to look up at the creature's massive head now standing almost three feet higher than her head. "I think I need a bigger gun."

Hell, she needed a bazooka! Or better yet, a tank. One thing was for sure, she needed something a hell of a lot bigger than what she was holding! Stumbling back a step, she almost sank to her knees when the creature made contact with the fencing lining the walkway.

The moment it did, lights flared and a protective dome appeared over the path she was standing on. Jordan's nose wrinkled when the scent of burning hair reached her. The creature howled in pain and jerked back down onto all six legs. With one last snarl, it disappeared back into the dark woods.

"And this… is why… you stay on the path," Jordan muttered in a shaking breath.

She slowly lowered her trembling arms back to her sides. Turning on legs that suddenly felt like rubber, she tucked the weapon back into her waistband and began jogging again, this time keeping a wary eye on the woods along the path. She made it to the park just as the transport arrived.

Crossing the deserted road, Jordan waved her credit chip over the scanner and waited for the door to slide open. Stepping in, she sank back against the plush seat. She set the backpack on the floor in front of her and withdrew her tablet.

"Forest Edge Eight-six-six-four-six, please," Jordan whispered.

She leaned back, clutching the tablet in her hand as the clear, oval-shaped transport rose into the air. Her eyes glanced down at the picture of Dagger that she had taken before he left. Tears glittered in her eyes, but she refused to let them fall.

Instead, she glanced out the window of the transport at the city far below. It appeared darker than the cities back home had because they used a red light that did not interfere with their night vision. Looking down at the array of lights, she could appreciate it even more when she glanced up at the stars. They were brilliant, much like the ones back on Earth after the lights had gone out. Only up at the cabin had she seen the stars this bright.

Somewhere out there was Dagger. Her *Amate*. He had promised when he finished his last assignment that he would come back to her, but he hadn't come back.

"I will wait until you are of age," Dagger's soft voice echoed through her mind. "But know this, Jordan Sampson, when you are old enough, you will be mine. I will claim you as my *Amate*. I will watch over you and protect you until then."

Jordan's fingers rose to touch her lips as she remembered the one and only kiss he had given her before he had left. He had pressed his lips to hers, and she had known that she was his. The kiss had consumed her and for the first time in her life, she felt... complete.

Looking down at the tablet, she focused on the information she had downloaded. Trig may have lost Dagger's tracks, but she hadn't. He had been sold and taken to the Tressalon galaxy. There were only a few Spaceports there, the biggest being Bruttus, which also happened to be the most deadly.

Gathering up her backpack, she watched as Dagger's home came into view. "You can stop here," she ordered. "I will walk the rest of the way."

"Please note the lighted pathways and remain on them," the transports automated voice replied. "Have a pleasant evening."

"I will, thank you," Jordan replied, stepping out of the clear transport once the door opened. "Please keep my destination private."

"Affirmative," the voice replied.

Jordan watched as the transport lifted off the ground again. Only when it was out of sight did she move down the path. Dagger's house was set several hundred feet back into the wooded area. There was a winding path leading to the front of it.

Walking along the soft surface of the path, she paused when she reached the outer security fence and saw the red glow of the security system. There were benefits to being the sister-in-law to one of the most powerful men in the city. One of them was hacking into his system at home without him knowing it.

Stepping up to the front gate, she laid her palm against the screen and anxiously waited while scanner read it. She had programmed her palm print into Dagger's security system not long after he was declared dead.

She had refused to believe that he wasn't coming back, and in her grief, had come to his house many times those first few months to be alone. A small part of her always hoped that he would somehow walk through the door. As the long weeks turned to months, she found refuge using his home as a place to quietly search for his location without fear of being interrupted.

She released a sigh of relief when the light turned green. *The last two years of intensive studying were finally paying off,* she thought.

Jordan pushed the gate open and stepped inside the courtyard. Shutting the gate, she waited for the security to reactivate. Now, she had one last major hurdle to conquer. She had to convince Dagger's older brother to take her along with him.

"No," she whispered. "It isn't the last one, but the beginning if… when he does."

Jordan straightened her shoulders and adjusted the backpack. She slowly walked up to the steps leading up to the front door. Her foot froze on the first step when a voice called out of the shadows to the left of her. A shiver ran through her body as she slowly turned to face the man she had come looking for. The man that could help her… if he believed her.

"Go home," Trig ordered, stepping out of the shadows.

Jordan's chin rose as she stared back at him. "No," she replied in a low voice.

"Go home, female," Trig said, walking past Jordan and climbing the steps toward the front door.

"I know where he is," she said, staring at Trig's stiff back.

She watched as he slowly turned to look at her with a dark scowl. For a moment, he looked so much like Dagger that pain pierced her. He must have smelled it, because he took a step toward her.

"Where?" He demanded, looking down at her.

Jordan returned the huge Trivator's stare with a cold determination. She would not allow Dagger to slip through her fingers. Slowly climbing the steps until she was just a couple of feet from him, Jordan pressed her lips together.

"I want to go with you to get him," she stated. "I will go with you."

Trig shook his head at her and started to turn away again. "Go home, female," he ordered. "This is no concern of yours."

"Yes, it is," Jordan retorted, grabbing his arm in desperation.

A low cry escaped her when he suddenly twisted. Jordan found herself pressed up against the wall next to the door, Trig's large hand curled around her throat. His eyes glowed a dark, menacing yellow as he leaned closer to her.

"I won't tell you again," he snarled under his breath. "Hunter needs to lock you up."

Jordan held still, refusing to look away from his intense gaze. "He's my *Amate*," she whispered. "He promised me he would come back, but he didn't. You had your chance and you lost him. The others gave up on him, but I never did. I know where Dagger is, Trig. I won't lose him again. Please," she begged quietly. "I can't lose. He... I can't lose him," she repeated.

The hand around her throat slowly moved away as he straightened and stepped back. Jordan refused to rub it. She wouldn't show any weakness that might cause Dagger's brother to change his mind about her going with him.

"Where is he?" Trig demanded in a rough voice.

Jordan stepped forward and kept her chin raised and her gaze steady. She had learned a lot over the last six years. First, how to survive back on Earth after the Trivator warriors appeared, and then more after Hunter brought her, Jesse, and Taylor to Rathon.

She had always been good with computers, mostly with gaming design, but that had changed after the Trivators appeared. After that, she studied programming and coding in case she ever needed it to protect her and her sisters. It had come in handy when Jesse needed to go after Hunter.

Once they were on Rathon, she had decided to continue her education. She used every ounce of the knowledge and skills she had learned over the past two years to locate Dagger after she read the reports from his crash. In her heart, she just couldn't accept that he was gone.

"Swear on your life that you will take me with you," Jordan forced out, ignoring the fierce scowl that darkened his face again. "I have to come with you. I can find him if they try to move him again. I know I can."

She knew she had won when Trig released a bitter curse and ran his hand down his face. With a grunt, he pushed past her and into Dagger's home. Jordan didn't wait, she turned and followed as he walked through the foyer to the living area.

Setting her backpack down on the floor next to the couch, she watched as he poured a drink from the small bar off to the side. He drained two small glasses of the brilliant amber liquor before he set the glass on the bar and turned to glare at her. Jordan bit her bottom lip, but couldn't quite keep the smile from curving her lips.

"What are you smiling about?" Trig asked, folding his arms across his chest and glowering at her. "I haven't said I'll take you with me."

Jordan gave him an exasperated sigh. "You look just like Dagger when he knows he isn't going to win the argument. And yes, you are. I was right about where he was last time. I was right about him being alive, and I'm right about him this time."

"I hate a female who is always right," Trig muttered with an envious glance at the almost full bottle of liquor. "Very well. I'll need to inform Hunter and set up extra security…." His voice died when he saw her face close up again and the same stubborn line pressed her lips tightly together. "What do *you* think we should do?"

Jordan bit her lip again and looked down at her hands. "I think we should leave tonight, now. Once we are on board your ship, I'll tell you where he is," she said quietly.

"How do you think Hunter will react to you disappearing with me? I'm not known for being nice," Trig replied in a dry, mocking voice.

Jordan looked up at him, staring back with an intensity that she knew took him by surprise. Her lips were pursed and she frowned back at him. She knew exactly how Hunter, and Jesse, would react. They had both been adamant that she understood they would stop her from doing anything crazy, like trying to go after Dagger. In her heart, she knew that Jesse would understand. After all, her older sister had done the same exact thing when Hunter had been taken.

Well, Jordan thought stubbornly, *I hope that she'll understand.*

Jordan knew her own personality. She always thought things through thoroughly before she did it. That was why she knew she could do this. All she needed to do was get to where Dagger was being held. She knew if she found him, she could figure a way to get him out.

It wasn't in her nature to be rash, but it also wasn't in her nature to ignore those she cared about because there was danger involved. She knew all too well what danger felt like.

"I know exactly who and what you are, Trig," Jordan responded in a cool, calm voice. "You work for a special division designed specifically to do the dirty jobs that the Alliance doesn't want anyone else to know about. You've been on twenty-four missions since your term of deployment with the Trivator military was completed three years ago. During those missions, you've lost two of your partners and swore to never have another; but, you've never lost the target you were sent in after. Would you like for me to detail each mission for you?" She asked, tilting her head and gazing back at him.

* * *

Trig's mouth tightened when he saw the familiar tilt to Jordan's head. It was like déjà vu of the night they left all over again. No, he had not needed her to give him a detail description of his missions. It was obvious that the human had somehow managed to get her hands on classified information and he seriously doubted that Hunter had just handed it to her.

"Are you sure?" He asked, briefly glancing down the alley at the passing residents.

He watched as she nodded. "Yes," she replied in a soft voice. "I saw... him."

"Where?" Trig demanded. "When?"

"He was in the fight ring." She lowered her eyes when tears filled them again. "They... Trig, I don't know how he has survived for so long," she said in a husky voice. "The other men... They had to kill each other and then this creature was released into the ring. Dagger killed it." A shudder ran through her body as she remembered what the creature did to not only the man in the ring, but to the woman outside of it. "The creature ate a man before it killed a woman who was watching outside of the ring. It tore her leg right off and no one bothered to help her. How can anyone do that to another living being. How, Trig?"

Trig's expression softened as he stared down at the emotion-filled eyes looking back up at him. He had come to respect this quiet human female over the last four weeks. She didn't talk much. She was always watching and listening to the things going on around her. She also spent every waking second going through the information she had filtered, searching for his brother.

Trig's hand rose and he gently touched her pale cheek. A sigh escaped him as he looked back at the pedestrians going about their daily life. She wasn't the only one who had done her homework. After he had finally answered Hunter's repeated communications, he had demanded that Hunter tell him about the human's background. He knew what Jordan's life had been like back on her own world.

"You shouldn't have gone there," Trig admonished in a soft voice, turning back to look at her. "Jordan, the situation has become too dangerous. It is going to be extremely difficult to get in and back out. If it had been Arindoss, I wouldn't think twice about going in alone, but I won't with a Dreluthan. They are a vicious and very dangerous species. It would be foolish to try to go up against one alone. I've sent a message to Hunter asking him for some assistance."

"I have two tickets to tonight's fight," she desperately interjected. She reached into the pocket of her cloak and withdrew the two inscribed pieces of metal. "We have to get him out of there, Trig, tonight, if possible. We have to."

Trig's admiration for Jordan increased when he saw the tickets in her hand. What struck him the most was that while her hand trembled, she had done something he had been unable to do for the past week. No one seemed to notice her as she moved about in the shadows. Perhaps it was because of the sense of frailty about her. She was not considered a threat. Unfortunately, he drew a lot of attention, even if he was known by many of the residents here on Bruttus.

"Come on," he said gruffly, reaching up and pulling the hood back over her head. "Let's go get something to eat and you can tell me what you found out."

He waited for her to nod and cover her face again before he moved back down to the entrance of the alley. Pausing briefly, he glanced one last time at her before they melted into the foot traffic of the Spaceport.

Chapter 4

Dagger shook off the bands around his wrists as the guards closed the gate behind him. Rolling his shoulders to ease the strain, he pushed back against the exhaustion that still plagued him. There was something different about tonight's fight. He could feel the tension in the crowds.

His eyes were fixed on the center of the cage. A large box stood in the center of the closed arena with two six-foot swords resting on it. His eyes scanned the other gated areas. There were no other opponents in them. Normally, there would be another fighter in each one, but tonight they stood bare.

A shiver of unease ran down his spine. He cautiously stepped into the arena when the gate in front of him lifted and the one behind him began to slide forward, forcing him into the dome-shaped enclosure. There would be no hiding from whatever 'fun' Kelman and the Drethulan had planned tonight.

The crowds cheered as he slowly moved toward the center. The lights had dimmed around them and a spotlight shone down on him as he approached the weapons. He turned in a half-circle, suspiciously scanning for a trap, before he turned and grasped the handle of a sword in each hand.

The moment he did, the spotlight shifted. He turned to where the light reappeared and released a silent cursed. The spotlight now shone down on his new opponent. How Kelman and the Drethulan managed to capture and transport a three-head Serpentian to the Spaceport wasn't his concern.

No, what worried him was he only had the two swords and no other opponent to distract its attention away from him. Rotating each sword in his hands, he checked the balance of them as he stepped backwards, his eyes glued to the enraged creature. Unlike the Gartaian that was almost blind, the Serpentian had excellent vision. The creature hissed, all three heads turned to follow him as he tried to put a little more distance between them.

Dagger's eyes flickered to the creature's sharp teeth, hard reddish-green scales, and foot-long claws that were digging into the metal floor. One of the heads reached out and gripped the thick, metal bar in its mouth, and began to pull on it. The fist-size iron bar groaned and bowed inward, a testament to the strength of the creature behind the bars. Within seconds, the other two heads gripped a different bar. The gate shook from the combined force pulling at it.

Silence descended among the spectators as they waited to see what happened next. Dagger ignored the silence, as well as the loud curses coming from the guards trying to open the gate. It proved an impossible feat due to the bent metal. Instead, they fell backwards when the railing holding the gate suddenly snapped.

Dagger ducked and rolled as the massive metal door flew through the air toward him. The Serpentian released a loud screeching sound as it moved out into the caged arena. The sound energized the audience who began to scream and yell. Dagger quickly climbed to his feet, warily watching as the creature moved along the perimeter of the arena.

His hands tightened around the grips of the swords and he stepped to the side. The movement pulled the Serpentian's attention away from the screaming masses and toward him. The muscles in his shoulders tensed as all three heads turned in his direction. The creature's pupils dilated and three sets of blood red eyes turned to focus on him.

Rage and determination burst through him when he saw the beast's muscles tense before it swirled around and charged him. Dagger released a loud war cry and sprang forward, raising one of the swords over his head while he kept the other close to his body. The fight had begun.

* * *

Trig pushed through the crowd trying to keep up with Jordan's small figure. He admired the way she gracefully moved through the packed corridor, weaving through the other spectators as if they weren't there. She did so with a quiet confidence that allowed her to blend until no one gave her a second glance. He wished he could say the same. There was no way to camouflage, who or what he was and he was definitely drawing some attention.

They had decided that it would be best if they appeared not to be together. Jordan had come through the entrance slightly behind him and in a different line. She was wearing the familiar dark brown cloak that covered her head all the way down to the tops of her dark brown boots. Light brown gloves covered her pale hands. He had given her a pair of dark goggles and a scarf to cover the majority of her face. She looked like one of the Sand people that inhabited the mining planets scattered throughout the star system.

He scowled when two guards walked toward him. His right hand instinctively tightened on the laser blade at his side. Only when they continued past him, did he relax his grip. He rounded the corner following the flow of the crowd toward the doors leading into the seating around the closed-in arena.

A frown darkened his face when he realized he had lost sight of Jordan. Unease rushed through him, and he moved closer to the wall as fans, eager to see the fight, pushed against him from behind. He started when he felt a light touch to his arm. Relief flooded him when he saw it was Jordan. She was standing in a small recess where a service access door was located.

He silently watched her wave a badge in front of the door before disappearing through it when it slid open. Pushing through behind her, he wondered how in the hell she had managed to get access. He took the steps leading up the narrow stairs two at a time and caught up with her on the second landing.

"How did you get a badge?" He asked curiously.

Jordan glanced over her shoulder and gave him a small smile. "I lifted it," she replied softly.

Trig touched her arm when she started to turn away. "They will be able to track the missing badge," he said with a frown. "It will trigger their systems when it is used."

Jordan shook her head. "No, it won't. I created a generic user when I printed out the tickets and dropped this one near the exit to the kitchen so it would appear that it was an accident. The new ID card will rotate through the system so it won't be flagged if I use it."

"How did you learn to do this?" He asked, puzzled.

Jordan shrugged her shoulders. "I've always been good at computers. I was a gamer before your people came to my world," she said in a soft, sad voice. "When... When Hunter took us away from it, I didn't know what would happen. I thought it would be important to know and understand how to use the technology on your world. It really became important to me when..." Her voiced faded for a moment. "Since Dagger disappeared, I knew I had to learn as much as I could so I could find him."

Trig's brow creased in confusion. "How did you know he was still alive?" He asked.

Jordan paused and a shadow crossed her face. "I couldn't believe anything else," she finally said, turning back around. "We can reach the third level through this access corridor. You were attracting too much attention."

Trig's gaze followed Jordan when she turned and proceeded up the stairs. She continued to amaze him with her resourcefulness. Following her, he waited as she stepped out and disappeared into the stand before he followed.

His eyes kept straying to Jordan's cloaked figure during the first two events. While he was used to the violence and ruthlessness of the fight rings, he worried about how Jordan would react to it. It was one thing to know that she had been to the one earlier, it was another to be there with her and see the viciousness through her eyes.

A cold determination filled him as he watched the second match. The crowd around him had been whipped into a bloodthirsty frenzy. The final two warriors struck at each other in exhaustion. It was obvious that they both wanted to quit, but they knew the only way that would happen is if one of them were to die.

"Kill him!" The spectator in front of him screamed. "Kill him! I've got twenty-five credits riding on this!"

The quiet determination coursing through him changed to an icy fury. The male standing in front of him only valued the life of those forced to fight for the measly twenty-five credits he had bet. Trig's fingers curled into fists to prevent him from reaching out and wrapping them around the male's neck. It would take two seconds to snap it. Unfortunately, it would be impossible to hide the act and would draw more attention to him than he was already attracting.

Instead, he was forced to act as if he was unmoved as one of the men in the arena stumbled backwards and fell. The move left him vulnerable to the heavy mace swinging toward him. The second fight might be over, but not without its casualties. The winner swayed for a moment before he collapsed from blood loss. Trig estimated the male would be dead in just minutes unless a healer was brought in and could stop the bleeding. At the rate the fighters were dying, the Drethulan would need a new supply. He would do everything he could to make sure that supply line was cut when he killed the bastard.

* * *

Jordan trembled, but remained silent as she watched the fight below her. It reminded her of the ancient Gladiators. How people could stand around and cheer such brutality was beyond her comprehension. She had watched movies on it and had even studied it in school, but real life was far different than Hollywood dramatizations or reading it in a book. The thought that Dagger had fought and survived for almost two years sent a shaft of pain through her. She would do anything and everything she could to free him from this place.

She gazed around as more and more people filled the already packed stadium. Seeing the push of bodies coming toward her, she quickly turned and climbed up and over the seats to the highest level. The next event was scheduled to start in fifteen minutes. The last thing she wanted to do was get caught in the crush of bodies. As small as she was, it wouldn't take much for her to get trampled. Working her way to the far end, she used the badge she had made and slipped through the locked doorway.

She made sure the door closed securely behind her before turning to the long ladder leading up to the top scaffolding above the stands. That was where she had stood earlier. She had to leave when another worker had come up to watch the fight as well. She hoped that no one else came up tonight. Grabbing the first rung, she began the long climb upward. There were eighty-seven rungs to the very top. Jordan counted each one, breathing deeply as she climbed. The excited cry of the audience as she neared the top swept through her and she increased her speed so she wouldn't miss what was happening. From the excited screams, she knew that Dagger had been brought out.

"Please, keep him safe," she whispered. "I just need time to get him out. Please give me the time to do that."

Stepping onto the top scaffolding with trembling legs, she moved through the shadows until she was even with the top of the half-domed cage. Her hand violently shook as she raised a gloved hand to her covered mouth. She barely smothered the cry of horror when she saw Dagger standing in the center of the arena. He wore a pair of dark brown leather trousers, dark brown boots and nothing else tonight. In his hands, he held two six foot swords.

Jordan's eyes roamed over Dagger's defiant form. The goggles Trig had given her allowed her to zoom in on him. Dagger's chest and arms were covered with deep scars from previous battles. She ignored everything, but the tall figure standing so fiercely before the screaming masses. Everything inside her willed him to win tonight's battle because she swore it would be the last one he fought if she could prevent it.

"Oh, God," she whispered when her eyes turned to his adversary tonight. "No!"

She watched in horror as the huge, metal gate flew across the center of the battleground below, barely missing Dagger as he rolled to the side. Silence descended throughout the fight-ring as the creature stepped out of the area holding it. Jordan leaned forward, wrapping her hands around the railing to keep from rushing down to Dagger. She knew any kind of a distraction would be fatal to him. Her chest hurt from where her heart was pounding as the creature turned and looked at Dagger. Her cry was lost in the screams of all the other spectators when Dagger released a war cry and rushed the creature.

"Dagger," Jordan whispered, unable to look away as the two deadly creatures collided.

* * *

Dagger swung the sword at one of the massive heads, twisting as a second one snapped at him. He rolled under the front foreleg of the beast, dragging one of the large swords along its breast before jumping to his feet. He barely had time to duck the tail that swung at him as it tried to twist around.

Using one hand, he braced it on the tail and jumped over it as it swept past him again. He had to roll again when one of the massive heads spun around to the left and snapped at him. Striking out, he caught a vicious blow to the right side of its head. The sword in his hand cut through the tender flesh just below the right eye of the Serpentian. The head snapped back, striking the one in the middle. He didn't have time to see what it did because the head on the left side was bent backwards, trying to reach him.

Twisting, he let the momentum of his body give him the strength he needed to slice through the thick greenish-red scales of the right neck. Satisfaction poured through him when thick, gooey green blood pumped from the deep gash across its neck. The head jerked backwards, but it was too late. The Serpentian's right head wobbled before falling forward.

The creature's scream shook the arena. Dagger stumbled backwards and shook his head as his ears rung from the loud, high-pitched sound. The Serpentian took advantage of his disorientation, striking him with its left head. He felt his feet leave the ground when the force of the blow picked him up as if he were little more than a child's toy. Pain exploded through him when he hit the thick bars of the cage before he dropped to the hard surface of the floor. He lost his grip on the sword in his right hand when he hit, and it skidded several feet away from him.

Clutching the sword in his left hand, he quickly rolled to the left when the Serpentian charged at him. It was off balance due to the weight of the dead head, but still just as deadly. He jumped to his feet and ran several feet before turning and holding the sword out in front of him. Instead of following him, the creature looked at him with one head while the other reached down and began gnawing at the lifeless head attached to its body.

Hoping for a chance to strike, he moved toward the massive body. The head watching him snarled in warning even as the other continued to tear at the flesh holding the dead head attached to its body. Dagger calculated that this was his best chance to attack. Rushing forward, he calculated the distance between him and the beast.

The moment the sharp teeth snapped at him, he swung the sword in a long, downward arc cutting through the flesh at the junction between the head and neck. What he hadn't calculated on was the speed at which the other head would strike back. Agonizing pain exploded through his shoulder when the middle head, its mouth dripping with dark green blood, shot out and bit down on his left shoulder.

The sword in his left hand was ripped away, buried in the neck of the creature. Darkness threatened to take him when the middle head of the creature lifted him up in the air. His body hung like a rag doll from its mouth. Dagger fought through the nausea and pain, refusing to admit defeat. Gritting his teeth, he swung his right hand up and into the creature's eye. His fist sunk into the soft tissue. Ignoring the feel of it, he dug his fingers into it and twisted. The massive jaw holding him by the shoulder, opened as the creature released a horrific screech of pain and fury.

He felt his body falling through the air before it landed with a sickening thump on the floor. He vaguely realized that he still held the eye of the Serpentian in his hand as he lay on the hard floor, warm blood soaking the ground under him. It took a moment for him to recognize that the crowd was chanting for him to finish the beast.

Dagger rolled, fighting the urge to just lie still. Crawling over to where the sword he had dropped earlier was lying, he wrapped his right hand around the grip. He used the sword to help him stand. Turning, he watched as the serpentine worked feverishly on trying to remove the second head.

Determination filled him as he shook past the pain and weakness threatening to take him. He would finish this tonight. He would be no man's pawn, especially Kelman or the Drethulan's, any longer. He would not be leaving the arena alive tonight if he had his way.

Stumbling forward, he released a loud roar. The Serpentian's head turned, the empty eye socket mocking him before it turned its head so it could focus on him. He stared back, his eyes devoid of emotion, at the blazing red eye.

"Freedom!" He roared, driving the sword up through the creature's jaw when it struck at him. "Freedom or death. Either way, I win this battle tonight!"

Twisting the sword in the tender flesh, he turned and stared up into the stands at Kelman, who had risen from where he was sitting in the third box reserved just for him. The arrogant bastard was smiling and slowly clapping his hands.

Dagger slowly withdrew the sword from the Serpentian's jaw and bared his teeth at Kelman before turning on the guards that rushed him. A primitive rage swelled inside him. Focusing that rage on the guards, he attacked them with a viciousness that left the audience in a frenzy.

Swinging the long sword, he tore through the first guard's chest before swiveling and burying it in the gut of the second guard. He was pulling it out when the first bolt of electricity hit him, causing him to stagger back. Unable to use his left arm, he wrenched the sword out as another bolt hit him. This one knocked him to his knees.

Dagger struggled to stand, but the sword was pulled from his grasp and he fell forward. His body bowed when another guard hit him with the stunner. Rolling onto his back, he stared hazily back toward Kelman. The bastard's smirking face looked down on him.

"Take him down and make sure he is patched back up," Kelman ordered. "I want him ready for the next fight."

"There's only the two fighters from earlier left," one of the guards grumbled. "Neither one of them can fight. Who else is he going to kill?"

Kelman's lips tightened into a knowing smile. "Perhaps more of his own kind," he stated. "If not, I'm sure you can be given to him to toy with. I want you to make sure the healer has him ready."

Dagger blinked back the darkness as it began to descend around him. Pain exploded through him when one of the guards grabbed his left arm so they could carry him out of the arena. He felt the last thin thread that separated him from the mindless fury of the Serpentian he had just killed, snap as the excruciating pain pulled him down into its inky darkness. The fragile link to his sanity had finally dissolved.

Chapter 5

Jordan blinked back the tears that blurred her vision. Tonight's fight had been horrifying. She had felt like her heart was being ripped out of her chest as she watched Dagger fight for his life. When the creature bit into his shoulder, she couldn't hold back her cry of anguish.

She saw Trig glance at her pale face in concern when she finally caught up with him. She wasn't the only one shaken by what she had seen. Trig's face was set in a cold, stony mask of determination and rage. Jordan had to force herself to walk away from the upper balcony and outside of the building. She knew that revealing her feelings could have devastating effects should anyone know that she was there for Dagger. She refused to become a pawn for those holding him captive. Instead, she kept her head down and focused on trying to get back to the room that Trig had rented for them.

She darted across the busy walkway to the other side. A dark corridor cut between two of the shops. The Spaceport was littered with the access corridors, allowing easy passage to the next section. Personally, she hated the dark corridors. They reminded her too much of the alley back on Earth where she had been attacked.

She pushed the choking fear down and stepped into the narrow passageway. Glancing over her shoulder, she saw Trig nod his head as he waited for her to go through first. Turning her head back to face the faint light at the other end, she picked up her pace.

Jordan breathed a sigh of relief when she rounded the corner, and leaned back against the wall of the corner shop. She had to duck her head to hide her face when two men walked past her into the alley. Curious, she turned to watch them. She bit back a cry of dismay when she saw Trig was fighting with a small group of men that must have come up behind him. There were at least five of them, not counting the two men who just entered the alley.

Hope blossomed inside her when she saw the two men that had passed her, rushed toward the struggling group. For a brief moment, Jordan hoped that they were going to help Trig, but instead, they joined in. She started to rush to help when she saw Trig suddenly collapse. One of the men had struck him in the back of the head.

Jordan pulled back and slipped between the panels of cloth hanging on display when the men started back toward her. The trembling that had started earlier grew when one of them paused at the entrance to the alley. She peeked through the material as another man approached from across the busy street.

"You get him?" The man asked.

"Yeah," the man from the alley replied. "Took him by surprise, but he still beat two of my men pretty bad. Even after I pumped him full of sedative to knock him out, he still wouldn't go down. I ended up hitting him in the head. Don't think it caused no damage."

"Deliver him to *The Hole,*" the man instructed. "This makes three Trivator warriors for the ring. Kelman and the Drethulan will pay big for them if they fight anything like the one he has now."

"Where's my credits?" The man demanded, shifting uneasily from one foot to the other. "I don't work for free."

Jordan watched as the man that had crossed the street withdrew a small purse. He pulled several slender chips and handed them to the scaled-faced man that had fought with Trig. She pulled further back into the shadows when he snorted and yelled out to the others to bring Trig forward.

"You'll get the rest when you deliver him," the man with the purse stated, watching as the other men carried Trig out of the alley.

Jordan quietly slipped from her hiding place and followed the small procession from a distance. Turning into the narrow alley across from the entrance to the fight ring, she bit her lip. Panic filled her as the realization that she was totally alone on an alien Spaceport washed through her. The only thing she had going for her was her brains.

One thing was for sure, she couldn't return to the apartment. It was too dangerous. The man had said they now had two more Trivator warriors. Trig had told her that he had asked for help. Surely, there would be more coming if the others didn't report back.

Glancing down the alley, she decided that the best plan of action was to learn where the men were being held inside *The Hole*. Once she knew that, she could look at the security systems. When the others came, she would be ready to help them. Until then, she would have to be extremely careful to not be caught.

* * *

A post on the outside of *The Hole* stated that it would be closed for the next two days. Jordan had heard that the Dreluthan who owned it wanted Dagger to be fully healed before he held another fight. In the meantime, the anticipation for the fight had gone viral across the Spaceport and more and more people were arriving to attend it.

Jordan took advantage of the pause between events to slip into the building and explore as much of it as she safely could. She had moved into a small abandoned room off the alley near the entrance to *The Hole*. It looked like it might once have been a side entrance to the business around the corner, but someone had sealed the doorway long ago. The area was just large enough for her to make a hiding place, and was close enough that she could monitor both the front and side entrance to the fight ring.

Slipping into the building using the badge she had made, she was crossing through the kitchen area when a rough hand grabbed her shoulder. Keeping her head down, she twisted under the pressure until she was facing a strange looking creature with a flat, orange face, no nose, and twin beady black eyes. A series of clicks and pops sounded when he spoke.

It took a moment for the translator in Jordan's ear to decipher what he was saying. Glancing up, she realized that it was one of the cooks. A frown creased her brow until she understood he wanted her to take the tray he was holding.

"Take this to the cell guard on Level Two," the cook ordered. "Then, make sure you wash the dishes."

Jordan glanced over at the mountain of dirty dishes stacked all along the counters and around the floor. She nodded and held out her hands to take the tray. A low hiss of breath escaped her as she turned away. This might be the chance she was searching for to break Dagger, Trig, and the other warriors mentioned out of wherever they were being held. All she needed to do was find a way to overpower the guard.

She had the small laser pistol that she took from Hunter's office. Swallowing, she carefully carried the tray through the winding corridors and down the steps to the lower level. It had been tricky a few times getting through the locked doors without dropping it. Whatever was on the plate was heavy and smelled horrible. This was one time she was thankful she had her nose and mouth covered.

Sliding her badge over the access panel, she waited as the door slid back before stepping through to the narrow set of stairs leading down. The steps wound around until they finally leveled out onto a short corridor. Jordan walked slowly, her eyes rising every few seconds to see what was in front of her.

She turned the corner and discovered a long hallway with a guard room at the far end. There was a single, solid metal door with a large window in it. On either side of the door were additional windows. The faint glow of a computer console lit the room, highlighting the guard sitting inside it.

Jordan continued down as the guard opened the door and scowled at her. Ducking her head, she trembled when she saw him rub the front of his pants and look down at her with a sly grin. She didn't need a translator to understand what the man was thinking.

"I haven't seen you before," the guard said, leaning back against the doorframe.

"Your food," Jordan replied in a husky voice. "Cook said to bring it."

"I could use some other sustenance as well," the guard replied, closing the door behind him.

Jordan thrust the tray out in front of her. The moment the guard took it, she stepped back several feet. Her hand started to slide toward her pocket where the laser gun was, but paused when she heard other voices coming from behind her.

Turning, she almost gave herself away when she saw the guards coming down the hallway carrying two other men between them. She immediately recognized them as Trivator warriors. Each had blood on their faces, a testament to the fight they must have put up.

Escaping back around the corner, she peered around it so she could watch where they took the two men. The guard opened the door and set the tray in his hand down before he pressed the panel inside. Her eyes flickered on the set of keys he also passed to one of the men. They used both electronic and manual locks.

She waited long enough to watch the door that opened beside the men. Turning away, she quickly climbed back up the stairs. Despair threatened to overwhelm her as her mind raced. She would need more than a little luck if she was going to overpower the guard, open the cells, and find the men before she was discovered as well.

"I'll need either a miracle or one hell of a diversion," Jordan whispered as she slipped back out of the building, bypassing the kitchens this time.

* * *

The miracle Jordan was looking for appeared the next day. She was just returning from a food run when she caught a glimpse of the dark-haired woman surrounded by Trivator warriors. She followed them through several sections, recognizing almost immediately where they were heading.

Making a quick decision, she knew she couldn't chance them getting caught as well. Weaving ahead of them, she waited until the dark haired human woman walked toward the stand where she was waiting. Jordan stepped out in front of her, blocking her way and drew in a deep breath. The woman started to step around in irritation before their eyes locked with each other. She started when she heard the woman's soft gasp and the faint sound of her name on the woman's lips.

"Jordan?" The woman asked in a husky voice.

Jordan's eyes widened and she nodded. A tiny, uncertain smile curved her lips as her eyes darted to the three men standing slightly behind the woman. Her hope for a miracle had been answered. Gripping her hands around her small cache of food. She motioned for the woman and three men to follow her.

"Yes, come with me," Jordan murmured in a low voice, glancing back and forth between them for a moment before she turned toward the alley.

A frown darkened her eyes when she glanced over her shoulder and saw one of the men in the group turn and hurry away. She watched, wondering if she was making a mistake trusting them. She pushed that fear away. All the Trivator warriors she had met so far had been kind and protective. The woman didn't appear to fear them. If anything, she had a look of determination in her eyes that Jordan completely understood.

Jordan waited until they followed her before pushing aside the long piece of fabric that she had hung over the recessed doorway. She heard one of the men caution the woman to wait until he made sure it was safe. Her confidence that she had made the right decision grew when he cautiously pushed aside the curtain and looked around the tiny space.

"Come," he called out, glancing briefly at Jordan. "Race, keep watch."

"Who are you?" Jordan asked quietly, staring intently at the woman's face. "Did Hunter send you?"

The woman shook her head and smiled. "No, I am here to find my *Amate*, Razor. My name is Kali Parks. This is Sword, the man outside is called Race, and the other guy that left is Cannon," Kali replied, folding her arms across her chest. "Razor was looking for you and Trig. Hunter did send him."

Jordan nodded in satisfaction. "I knew Hunter would be worried. I had to come. Dagger... Dagger has been lost for too long. After... after seeing what he has been through, I can't leave him now that I've found him again," she forced out in a voice thick with tears.

The tears Jordan had been holding back escaped her when Kali touched her arm. She didn't resist when Kali wrapped her arms around her in support. For several long moments, Jordan drew strength from knowing she wasn't alone in her fight to free the men.

"It will be alright. We'll get them all out. I was going to go have a 'talk' with Arindoss," Kali whispered.

Jordan pulled back and shook her head. She wiped at her damp cheeks and nervously glanced at Sword who was standing silently by the door, listening to everything. Releasing a shaky breath, she wound her arms around her waist.

"Arindoss is dead. Trig and I saw one of his security guards turn on him in the lower markets. Shortly after he was killed, a strange looking creature came and ordered the man to get rid of the body,"

Jordan said, biting her lower lip at the memory. She haltingly explained what happened and described the Drethulan to Sword when he asked what the man who now owned *The Hole* looked like. "His eyes are large and black with no emotion in them. His skin is hard, with a yellowish tint, and has touches of black and red in it. I've heard him called by several different names. He is a horrible creature."

"A Drethulan," Sword cursed.

Jordan nodded, that had been one of the names she had heard. "He is the one that has been bringing in the creatures for those... for the fighters. He said it is more exciting and profitable, according to the information he has been sending out," Jordan whispered. "Dagger and two other men are the only ones who have survived the fights so far this week."

"He will need to replenish his fighters," Sword commented, glancing at Kali who nodded in agreement.

"From what I've seen in the past couple of days, the... Drethulan, has been sending teams of men out to find new fighters. Two days ago, they attacked Trig."

"That may be why they attacked Razor and Hammer," Sword replied, rubbing his chin as his brow furrowed in thought. "Trivator warriors are fierce and will fight to the death."

Jordan glanced back and forth, the sense of hope growing at the same time as a smile curved Kali Parks' lips. The devilish gleam in them was her first warning that the woman was up to something.

"Jordan, how good are you at sneaking around?" Kali asked, looking at her with a thoughtful expression. "Can you get inside *The Hole* unseen?"

"Yes, I've been searching for Dagger and Trig. I stole an access key from one of the kitchen workers to get in originally. I've created a generic pass so I can move in and out without difficulty," Jordan replied with excitement. "I have a good idea of where they are being kept."

Jordan pulled the small tablet she had brought from home out of the pouch hanging at her waist and swiped her finger over it. She tapped in several codes, pulling up a schematic of the huge complex.

"This is the floor plan of the interior," Jordan said, glancing at the diagram. "There are a few changes from the original design. I've marked those in red."

"Where did you get this?" Sword asked in surprise, gazing down at the holographic image.

Jordan briefly glanced up at him and smiled. "I hacked into the Space Station's building archives," she murmured. "There are three levels under the complex that are used to hold the fighters. The first one isn't in use right now. The second and third one are. I think that's where they are holding the men."

Kali's soft laughter filled the tiny room as she stared down at the image Jordan was displaying. "Jordan, you are a genius," she exclaimed.

Jordan raised troubled eyes to Kali and shook her head. "No, I'm desperate. I've been studying and learning the coding so that I could find Dagger. He's there. I have to help him before… before they put him back into that cage again," she whispered in a barely audible voice.

"We will," Kali assured her. "I have a plan."

Jordan's eyes flickered to Sword when he winced at Kali's words. She glanced back down at the image in her hands. Tears burned in the back of her eyes. She rapidly blinked, pushing them away. Tears could come when Dagger was safe. Then, she would cry, but it would be tears of happiness instead of sorrow.

Chapter 6

Dagger rolled until he was in a crouching position. He had been shot with a tranquilizer dart twenty minutes before. It was the only way the healer could check to make sure his wounds were healed. The guards knew that if they tried to enter the cell without him being sedated, that someone was going to die. Unfortunately for the guards, Kelman made sure they knew it wouldn't be Dagger. No, he was far too valuable to Kelman and Talja. Instead, they knocked him out.

Dagger listened as the healer muttered incoherently and clutched the few supplies he had against his chest as he scurried from the cell. A low, steady burning coursed through his system. He knew it was the remains of the drug the healer had shot into the vein of his neck. Rolling his head from side to side, he gritted his teeth and ignored the familiar burning sensation of the drug.

Instead, he focused on Kelman. His eyes followed the pale figure of the mercenary as he stepped just inside the cell. Pulling on the chains restraining him, he flashed his teeth at the other male in warning. His eyes flickered to where Kelman leaned down to pick up a piece of white hair off the floor.

"I kept the strands cut off from when I bought you," Kelman said, rolling the short pieces of white hair between his fingers before letting them fall to the floor. "A shame that it was necessary to cut it."

Dagger didn't respond. The fact that his hair had been cut short soon after his capture meant nothing to him. The fact that Kelman kept it did. It was another way the mercenary thought he owned him. The muscles in Dagger's arms bulged as he strained to break loose of the chains holding him.

Kelman glanced at the guards standing warily outside the cell. "Make sure he is fed. I want him ready for the next fight. He will be facing two of his own kind," Kelman ordered with a chuckle. "Talja has outdone himself this time. He has three more. If you die, I will at least have a replacement."

Dagger's head bent forward as he wrapped his hands around the chains and stood up. The sound of the metal creaking and groaning had Kelman stepping backwards several feet until he was safely through the door. The guard closest to him quickly stepped forward and slammed the thick door shut just as one of the links in the chain broke.

Dagger didn't wait. Swinging the long chain out, he caught the guard under the chin. The force of the blow shattered the man's jaw. The guard's body flew backwards into another guard that had moved in front of Kelman.

He pulled the chain back into the cell, winding it around his palm. Kelman's mocking laughter echoed through the dark corridor. The mercenary was smart enough to move away from the cell.

"Knock him out," one of the guards yelled.

"No," Kelman ordered. "Leave him. Send for more food. I don't want anything to slow him down."

"How are we supposed to feed him if we can't get close to the cell?" The guard demanded, glancing warily at Dagger before turning his gaze to Kelman. "What does it matter anyway, he hasn't touched the last tray we left him."

"Figure it out," Kelman replied with a shrug. "I don't want anything to slow his healing. There is a match scheduled for tomorrow night. I want you to make sure he is ready for it, otherwise you will be taking his place."

The guard grumbled under his breath, but didn't say anything else to Kelman. Nodding to the other three guards with him, they each grabbed a limb of the unconscious guard and picked him up. The guard glanced at his comrade's gaping, oddly-twisted jaw.

I'll feed the Trivator, he thought with a nasty grin. *I'll feed him the remains of the Serpentian.*

Dagger watched them leave. Soon, darkness swallowed him in its shadows once again when all but one set of lights were turned off. He turned and braced his legs on the floor. Wrapping both hands around the chain holding his left wrist, he pulled. Only when he felt the satisfying give of one of the links and was able to wrap the chain around the palm of his left hand did he turn back around.

He would be ready for the next guard who made the mistake of coming into his cell. He would kill them without mercy. Shifting backwards, he allowed the shadows to hide him once again from the view of the cameras.

* * *

"This way," Jordan said in a low voice. "There is one guard at the far end. He runs the controls for the lower levels."

Jordan hoped Kali's plan worked. Kali and Cannon, along with three other species Cannon had returned with, were going to create a distraction while she and Sword found the others and released them.

Sword scowled down at her and his lips tightened as if he already knew he wasn't going to like the answer she was going to give him. "How do you know that?" He asked.

"I delivered food to him yesterday," she responded quietly.

"You...." Sword started to say before the scowl on his face turned even darker. "Stay here," he ordered.

Jordan turned and pressed her hand against his chest. "No, I'll go. He will sound the alarm if you do. I'll take care of him," she whispered, turning to pick up a discarded tray and cup from the floor.

They were too close to succeeding to take a chance of something going wrong. She ignored the trembling in her hands as she reached into her pocket and pulled out the laser pistol. There was no way she would allow Dagger to suffer any more.

Turning the corner, she ignored Sword's angry hiss. Her stomach turned over when the guard from yesterday stood up and grinned when he saw her walking toward him. He slowly stretched before he opened the door and watched her with greedy eyes.

Her fingers tightened around the small laser pistol. She refused to think about what she was about to do. Instead, she focused her thoughts on Dagger.

Jordan vaguely knew she was answering the man's questions, she could only hope the responses made sense because all she could think of was that she was about to shoot another living being. Dropping the tray, she raised the laser pistol in her hands and fired. Horror swept through her when she realized that her hands had been shaking so badly that she missed.

A gasp escaped her when the gun was suddenly ripped from her hands and a hand wrapped around her throat, lifting her up off the floor. Jordan's hands grabbed at the beefy wrist cutting off her air. She fruitlessly clawed as the fingers tightened even more. Her lungs began to burn and darkness began to fog her vision.

"You shouldn't play with weapons if you don't know how to use them," the guard growled.

Jordan tried to kick out at the guard, but it was useless. She could feel her muscles beginning to relax and her hands fell to her side as the lack of oxygen took its toll on her. Pain exploded through her when the guard slammed her back against the wall. She couldn't understand what he was saying over the buzzing in her ears.

Relief flooded her when the hand around her throat suddenly vanished. Unable to stand, she slid down the wall. She watched as Sword turned the body of the guard around and sliced the blade in his hand across the guard's neck. Her hands went to her throat and she closed her eyes when blood splattered outward.

Jordan swallowed and rubbed at her bruised throat. She released a low cry and jerked when warm hands tenderly gripped her forearms. Her eyes popped open, her pupil's dilated with fear, as she stared up at Sword.

Sword stared down at her with concern. "Are you alright?" He asked quietly.

Jordan nodded before forcing the words pass her tender throat. "Ye... yes, tha... thank you," she choked out hoarsely.

Jordan grasped the hands held out to her and allowed Sword to help her to stand. Turning, she kept her eyes diverted from the body of the guard.

"There are no other guards that I could tell from here on. The guard here controlled the locking mechanisms to each section," Jordan whispered.

Sword nodded, stepping into the room that the guard left open. "I will take care of it," Sword instructed. Jordan watched as he tapped through the security system. "I've found them. I'll go to level two and release Razor, Hammer and Trig first."

"Have you... What about Dagger?" She asked.

Sword glanced at Jordan's worried face. "He is in the last cell on the left on the third level," Sword replied. "I won't leave him."

Jordan's gaze turned to the screen on the panel. Only Dagger's hands were visible in the grainy resolution. Relief and determination filled her. The thought of being so close to him, yet still apart tore through her. For the past two years, this had been the total, consuming goal in her life. Now, it felt almost surreal.

"I'll go release him," she murmured, her eyes glued to the screen.

Sword turned and gripped her shoulders in a gentle grasp. He stared down at her with a look of hesitation, as if trying to determine what he should say next. She turned her eyes to his shuttered gaze, knowing instinctively that he was trying to protect her feelings.

"I don't want you down there alone, Jordan," Sword stated firmly. "Dagger has been held for over two years. He… he might not be sane after what he has been through. It might be necessary to knock him out."

Jordan's eyes turned to the screen. She watched as Dagger stepped into the dim light and glared at the camera, as if he knew that they were talking about him. Her gaze ran over the long scar that ran along his right cheek before locking on the cold hatred in his eyes. A part of her knew that Sword was right, but another part knew that Dagger would never hurt her. He needed her, just as she needed him. She had made a promise to him two years ago, that if he didn't come back, that she would find him. She had kept her promise.

No, he would not hurt me, she thought with confidence. *If anything, I might be the only one who can reach through the hatred.*

"Go, do what you have to," she murmured in a soft voice. "I'll make sure that you aren't trapped down there."

Sword paused, unsure whether he should leave her or not. Finally making a decision, he nodded. "Stay here. Lock the door in case anyone comes. I will return in ten minutes," Sword ordered and stepped out of the room.

Jordan's eyes flashed over the dead body of the guard before returning to Sword. "I'll be okay. Go. I want to get out of here," she assured him. "Just… free them."

Sword nodded again, closing the door behind him. Jordan waited until he was near the door with the spare set of keys that had been in the room. She pressed the button to release the first set of locks. Within seconds, he had inserted the key and disappeared down the stairs to the next level.

Her eyes flashed to the screen where she could see Dagger still staring up at the screen, almost as if he was willing her to come to him. Making a decision, Jordan opened all the doors leading down before short-circuiting the system. The smell of burning wires made her nose sting.

She turned and opened the door to the guard room. Swallowing back the nausea, she shut the door and walked over to the dead guard. He had his set of keys still attached to his waist. She knelt down and yanked them off before standing again. Her eyes swept the darkened recesses for the laser pistol he had taken from her. Spying it up against the wall, she hurried over and picked it up.

She cast one last look at the screen through the window of the guard station before firing a single shot into the door panel, sealing it closed. A wave of calm washed over her as she inserted her key into the door. The moment it opened, she stepped through and headed down the stairs.

Chapter 7

Dagger tensed at the sound of footsteps coming down the steps. They were softer, lighter than the normal heavy steps of the guards. He moved back into the dark, waiting and watching. It may be a servant bringing the food Kelman had ordered. Whoever it was, if they came close enough to the cell, he would kill them.

He froze as the keys clattered and the lock clicked. A menacing smile curved his lips. It might be a trap, but he didn't care. He highly doubted that Kelman would allow an unprotected servant to bring the food. To date, only the guards had delivered it, and never alone. There was always a minimum of five or more.

His suspicion that it was a trap intensified when a small, cloaked figured moved quickly down the corridor without turning on any additional lights. He silently waited, studying the figure. There was something oddly familiar about it, something that tugged at his consciousness, telling him that he shouldn't strike out.

He ruthlessly pushed the feeling away. Gripping the chains clenched in his hands, he watched as the figure briefly paused to look over his shoulder before pushing the key into the lock. The moment the door swung open, he released the chains.

A harsh gasp escaped the hidden form as the twin chains wrapped around its body. Dagger jerked on the thick metal links, pulling the stunned figure toward him. His hands wrapped around the fragile wrists that shot out as it tumbled forward.

Twisting, Dagger jerked the arms up. A low growl escaped him when he saw the laser pistol in one of the gloved hands. He pressed his thumb against the nerve along the wrist, forcing the hand open. The laser pistol clattered to the floor next to his foot. With a slight kick, it slid away from where they were standing.

"You should have used that before you came in," he snarled in a low, icy voice. "How many are waiting for me?" He demanded, brutally increasing the pressure around the wrists.

"Dagger," a soft, familiar voice whispered.

The husky voice seared through the haze of hatred, for a moment paralyzing him. He shook his head in confusion. He shifted until he was holding both wrists in one hand. Reaching down, he roughly pulled back the hood of the cloak hiding the face of the figure.

Dagger's mind rebelled, trying to reason that this had to be a trick or a product of his imagination. The last thought disintegrated to ash when the illusion of Jordan rose up far enough to press her lips against his. A shudder ran through him and a low groan escaped him at the soft, tender touch.

The hand holding her wrists opened and dropped so he could pull her closer. He deepened the kiss, desperately clutching her warm body against his. His hands tightened on her waist, his fingers curling into her soft flesh as he fought for control.

Jordan's slight whimper told him that he was holding her too tight. She was real, not an illusion of his fractured mind, but a solid, warm, breathing and living Jordan.

Dagger reluctantly pulled back. He gazed down at her in confusion. His splintered mind tried to comprehend the reality of her presence in the cell, in his arms, when he had finally accepted that she had been nothing more than a figment of his imagination. Lifting one trembling hand, he buried it in her hair.

"How did you…? Kelman," he started to say in a rough, disjointed voice. "You shouldn't be here. It is too dangerous."

Jordan shook her head and glanced behind him with a worried look in her eyes. "We have to get out of here. Sword is releasing the others that were captured. We have to get out of here before the Dreluthan and Kelman know what is happening."

A primitive rage rose up at the same time as a renewed determination settled over him. This time, though, instead of the desire to find and kill Kelman and Talja, he was focused on getting Jordan as far away from here and the two men as possible. He looked down at where Jordan was unlocking the wristbands from his around his wrists. He let them fall to the floor. She quickly sank down and undid the ones around his ankles.

Dagger kicked the chains away from him and stepped back, energized at the release of the manacles. He silently wrapped his hand around Jordan's right wrist and pulled her back to her feet.

Still holding her arm, he turned and strode over to where he had kicked the pistol.

Dagger scooped the small weapon up and checked the charge. It registered full. Twisting, he pulled Jordan behind him as he strode out of the cell. A fragmented part of his mind registered that he needed to be gentle with her, that in the state of mind he was currently in, he could easily hurt her without meaning to.

"Others?" Dagger asked in a harsh voice, moving toward the stairs leading up to the next level. "Who are they?"

"I came here with your brother, Trig," Jordan said in a hushed voice. "He was captured two days ago. The Drethulan has been sending men through the Spaceport looking for fighters. Another group of Trivator warriors arrived earlier this morning when two of their men disappeared. Sword, one of the Trivator warriors who arrived, has gone to free Trig, a man named Razor, and another man. I... I can't remember his name, Kali told me, but I forgot."

"Trig... Razor?" Dagger growled with a frown, trying to comprehend what was going on. He shook his head, which felt like it was in a fog. His thoughts were disorganized, scattered, making it difficult to understand what Jordan was telling him. "What about the guards?"

Jordan shook her head and bit her lip. "Kali and several others were creating a diversion. There weren't any other guards down here when Sword and I came down, just the one..." Her voice faded as she remembered the dead guard. Clearing her sore throat, she pushed everything but the need to escape from her mind. "I have a badge to get us through the building. We are to meet up with a warrior named Race. He is supposed to have a ship ready."

Dagger paused at the foot of the stairs. "Others come," he growled, sniffing the air.

* * *

Panic gripped Jordan. She pulled loose from the hold Dagger had on her wrist and reached for the tablet with the blueprint of the building on it. Swiping her finger across, she pulled up the diagram. Her eyes swept the area. She turned away from the stairs leading up.

"This way," she said in a low voice. "There is another exit near the cell where you were at. This level was not originally equipped to handle the cells, but was designed for storage and access to the underground utility tunnels, probably for smuggling."

Dagger's gaze moved to the holographic image, then back to Jordan's face. He finally glanced over his shoulder before he nodded. While he wanted to fight and kill the ones that had caged him, it would have to wait. Jordan's safety was paramount to everything else.

"Can you unlock the door?" He asked, pulling her back the way they had come.

"Yes, the badge I have should work. I gave it full access," she replied.

"Go," he said, turning with a low growl as four guards pushed through the door. "Go!"

Jordan's eyes widened in terror, but she did as he told her. Pulling the badge out of her pocket, she almost dropped it when a blast of laser fire burned into the metal next to her head. Swiping the door, she groaned when she realized it also needed a key.

Her hand froze and her eyes darted back to the cell. She had left it in the manacle when she unlocked the last leg restraint. She slid the tablet into her pocket and darted out from behind Dagger. A low cry escaped her when one of the guards opened fire.

Jordan tripped over the tray of untouched food and fell hard on the cold, metal floor. Crawling on her hands and knees, she struggled for a moment to get the key out of the lock. Her head swiveled to look back at where Dagger was still firing on the guards, well, guard. There were three bodies lying about the man standing at the far end.

She watched as the man fell back, a dark patch spreading across the front of his chest. He slid down the wall as if in slow motion, his arms falling to his side. Rising up, Jordan stumbled out of the cell to where Dagger was kneeling. She fell to her knees beside him, hurriedly searching him for wounds.

"You're bleeding," she whispered, touching his bare shoulder before her hands fluttered to his side. "You've been hit in several places."

"Minor wounds," he growl, jerking his head toward the door. "Can you open it?"

"Yes," she said, standing up and helping him to his feet. "It… I needed the keys to open it."

"Hurry," Dagger ordered through gritted teeth. "More are coming."

Jordan nodded. Swiping her badge again, she inserted the key and pulled the door open. Her head jerked when she heard a deep voice calling out Dagger's name. Turning, she stared in horror at the glittering cold eyes of Cordus Kelman. Instinctively, she took a step closer to Dagger's stiff form.

"Trivator!" Kelman yelled from the end of the corridor. "You'll never escape."

Dagger's eyes narrowed and his mouth tightened into a straight line. Jordan felt his arm pull her behind him and toward the open door. With a cold, calmness that amazed her, Dagger raised the pistol in his hand.

"Kelman," Dagger snarled. "You are a dead man."

Jordan noticed Kelman's eyes flickered briefly from Dagger to her before returning to Dagger. She stepped closer to the open door, not wanting to hinder Dagger in any way. She noticed that Dagger's eyes were glowing with a fierce, yellow-gold color. She had never seen them like this before.

"You have a female," Kelman remarked, glancing at Jordan's delicate pale coloring. "She is… unusual."

Dagger's enraged snarl echoed through the long corridor. Instead of replying, he pressed the trigger on the pistol. Jordan's gasp of dismay was lost in the mocking laughter that echoed when nothing happened. The pistol's charge was depleted.

Jordan watched in horror as Kelman motioned for the guards standing slightly in front of him to move forward. She could feel the tension in Dagger's body building as he prepared to fight them. Something inside her snapped at the idea of losing him again. She couldn't do it.

Grabbing Dagger's arm, she pulled him toward her and through the open doorway. Laser fire erupted, lighting up the area around them. She cried out in pain when one of the blasts sliced across her arm as she pulled the door shut behind them.

"Destroy the panel," she cried out, shoving the key into the lock on the inside of the door.

Jordan ignored Dagger's low, guttural curse. She heard the sound of shattering glass as he used the butt of the empty pistol against the panel. Soon, the familiar smell of burning wires touched her nose again, making her want to sneeze. Shaking her head and wiggling her nose, she worked at breaking the key in the lock.

"Let me," Dagger grunted, pushing her to the side.

Jordan nodded and stepped back. Her arm was stinging and she could feel the sticky dampness of blood against her skin. She started when she heard the slight sound of metal on metal as Dagger threw the broken piece of the key to the side.

"This tunnel has multiple exits," Jordan whispered, staring at Dagger with wide, worried eyes. "We need to get to the far end. It will split into two different directions from there. If we take the one to the left, it should lead us back into the Spaceport."

"Where does the right one go?" He asked, looking down the corridor lined with coolant, electrical, and environmental piping.

Jordan jumped when she heard the sound of banging on the other side of the door and moved closer to Dagger. "It is an emergency release. It leads outside of the Spaceport."

"Let's go," Dagger said, reaching out to grab her arm.

Jordan cried out when his fingers wrapped around where she had been shot. The protest died on her lips when she saw the look of worry and rage in Dagger's eyes. Biting her lip, she tried to stop him from pulling back the sleeve of her cloak.

"It's just a scratch," she insisted. "We need to leave before they find a way to open the door. There are almost a dozen corridors leading off the branch of tunnels to the upper levels of the Spaceport. It will be difficult for them to find which one we use. We need to get to the Spaceship that Kali said would be waiting for us."

Jordan touched Dagger's chin with her free hand, turning it toward her when he snarled under his breath at the long, blistering wound on her right forearm. She rubbed her thumb along his smooth jaw.

Dagger's eyes darkened with frustration and concern as he stared down at her. She could still see the confusion and suspicion in his eyes, as if he wasn't sure that any of this was real. Her eyes touched on the long scar running from the corner of his right eye down to just before his upper lip. It was another testament to what he had gone through.

She pulled in a startled breath when he leaned forward and pressed a brief, hard kiss against her lips before stepping back and turning away. Her hand rose to touch her tingling lips and her expression softened when he diverted his gaze from her as he pulled back. There was a lot more in that kiss than Dagger realized. She could almost taste his confusion, vulnerability, and fear in it. Slipping the tablet back into her pocket, she silently followed him.

Chapter 8

Dagger's eyes swept back and forth as they moved down the narrow corridor. His mind was reeling at the knowledge that Jordan was here, on Bruttus. Instinctively, his hand reached out behind him. He didn't turn his head to look at her. A small part of him was afraid if he did, he would discover this was all a dream and she wasn't real. An explosion of emotion swept through him when he felt her slender fingers wrap around his.

He curled his around them and was rewarded with a slight squeeze. He slowed as they neared the end of the corridor. She had been right, it did fork.

"The right will take us to the Spaceport," she murmured.

His eyes scanned the brightly lit corridor that curved around before he turned his head to look down the left one. It was dark. His head whipped around and a low snarl escaped him when he heard the faint sound of footsteps moving down the right tunnel toward them.

"Go left," he ordered, glancing behind him and over her head. "They are coming."

"We're trapped," she whispered, feeling sick to her stomach. "Maybe Sword and the others will come."

"Go," Dagger replied, gripping her hand firmly in his, and pulling her toward the left. "We cannot wait for them."

He knew his brother and Razor well enough to know that they could take care of themselves, especially if other warriors were helping. Besides, right now, he would probably kill them all for allowing Jordan to be here. He would start with his brother, Trig, and work his way through them. Until that time, his only concern was to keep Jordan safe.

He slowed his pace slightly when Jordan stumbled. The darkness of the tunnel wasn't an issue for him, but it was for her. He needed to remember that humans could not see as well in the dim light.

"There is a door up ahead," he whispered. "Stay against the side. I will see what is beyond it."

Jordan nodded and slipped to the side, trying to make herself as small and motionless as possible. Already, Dagger missed the warmth of her touch. Forcing himself to step away, he strode on silent feet toward the door. A small narrow window in the center allowed him to see what was behind it.

Surprise and satisfaction burned through him when he saw a *Lexamus IV* Class Starship. They were top of the line, fast and very maneuverable ships favored by the elite pirates and smugglers. Something told him that this one had belonged to Arindoss.

His hand moved to the panel. He glanced back at where Jordan stood pressed against the wall. Her head was bowed and she was holding her wounded arm close to her body.

"Jordan," he called softly.

Her head jerked up and she pushed away from the wall. He didn't miss the slight movement of her hand as it brushed against her cheek. When she stepped up to him, he could see the faint traces of moisture from her tears.

"I am going to kill Trig when I see him again," he murmured, gently touching her pale cheek. "He should have known better than to bring you here."

A shy, tired smile curved Jordan's lips as she looked up at him. "I didn't exactly give him much of a choice," she admitted before turning to look at the panel. Pulling the badge she had made out of her pocket, she swiped it over the access panel. The faint red light continued to blink. "It's not working."

Dagger looked down at her before glancing over his shoulder. They were about to have company. He needed to give her time to get through the door. He turned back as she pulled the tablet she had earlier out and swiped her finger across it. Her fingers flew over the screen.

"Get the door open, Jordan. The moment it is, get inside and seal it again," Dagger ordered, turning away from her.

Jordan's head jerked up and her eyes widened. "Where are you going?" She asked.

"To give you time," Dagger whispered, turning back and touching her cheek with the tip of his fingers. "Get inside."

Jordan turned her head and pressed her lips to his fingers as they slid across her skin. "I'll open it, but you'd better come with me, Dagger. I swear I'll come after you again. I'll always come after you."

Dagger's eyes burned with emotion. He turned away, letting the cold rage and deadly skills he had perfected over the last two years guide him. Disappearing back the way they came, he sniffed the air. There were three different scents. His eyes glowed before his eyelids lowered to conceal them.

Scanning the darkness, he picked out a space in the upper conduits. He jumped up and grabbed the cold metal lines and pulled himself up. He twisted around, planting his feet at the support bracket holding the lines in place. His left shoulder burned from the still healing wound and the new ones he had received earlier, but he ignored them. The pain had become his friend over the last two years. He used it to help him focus on those that had inflicted it.

He watched as the three men paused at the intersection between the junction. One glanced toward the darker area where he was while the other two looked back down the long corridor leading back to the cells.

"This way," one of the men said, jerking his head toward the corridor leading to the cell. "They must not have got this far."

"What about that area?" The man next to him said, nodding toward the darkened tunnel. "They could have gone that way."

"It's a dead end," the third man grumbled. "The map I got says it leads outside. Unless they got suits, they can't get out. Besides, if they had opened the door, we would've known."

"How?" The second man asked, frowning at the dark corridor.

The third man shook his head and moved away from the opening toward the long, lit corridor. "Cause it would have sucked us out into space," the man snapped.

"I think they made it to the first exit," the first man grumbled under his breath. "I don't want to deal with that Trivator. I've seen him fight."

"So have I," the third man retorted, holding his laser rifle tightly against his shoulder. "Why do you think I'm not going down any dark corridors? If you want to check it out, you go."

"Kelman says we have to check every section," the second man defended. "He said if we let him get away, he'll put us in the cage next."

"Yeah, well, being dead here or being dead there isn't much of a choice, is it?" The third man pointed out. "I say we go down this passage. If it is clear, we will meet up with the other group. They should have blasted the door by now. If not, then the Trivator will be trapped between us and we have a better chance of making it out of this alive. If not, we did what we were ordered to do, we checked it out. He must have made it to the first exit before we got down here."

The second man looked back at the dark section again with indecision. He had seen the Trivator fight too. In fact, he had lost money on the last bet two nights ago. He thought for sure the Serpentian would have defeated the fighter. Still, if he had to go up against one or the other, he would almost rather face the Trivator, at least he would die quickly instead of slow like he had seen Kelman or the Drethulan kill those that defied them.

"I'll check it out," he grumbled unhappily. "It isn't that far and I don't want Kelman finding out."

The first man shrugged. "Fine," he said. "I'm with him. Make it quick and catch up. We're going to head toward the door."

Dagger's eyes narrowed on the overweight guard. The male should have listened to his comrades. He waited until the guard had walked under him before he dropped down silently behind him. He needed the weapons the male was carrying.

The guard must have sensed the danger or had second thoughts about checking the corridor because he turned just as Dagger landed. His eyes widened in surprise and his hand holding the laser pistol rose to fire.

Dagger grabbed the guard's wrist, twisting it to the side as it discharged. At the same time, he turned and wrapped his arm around the man's neck. The other two guards, alerted by the laser fire, rounded the corner at the same time firing. The burst of fire struck the guard Dagger held in the chest, shoulder, and stomach. Fortunately for Dagger, the guard was a large male and shielded his body from the bursts.

Gripping the guard's hand, he forced the man's finger down on the trigger. He hit one of the guards in the forehead, sending the man flying backwards into the brightly lit corridor. The other guard, realizing what he was facing, started to back up as he continued to lay down fire.

Dagger dropped the dead guard in his arms. He quickly twisted the pistol out of the man's limp fingers and moved forward. He held the pistol steady, waiting for the guard to lean around the corner again.

He didn't have long to wait. The guard rolled across the floor, firing as he did. The male, expecting Dagger to have remained in the center of the corridor didn't realize that Dagger had moved closer to the side until it was too late. The guard's eyes widened as a hole opened up in the center of his chest. The male's head fell backwards and his eyes glazed over even as his head fell backwards.

Dagger didn't waste any time. Moving swiftly over to the guard at the entrance to the corridor, he removed the weapons from his hand and those at his waist. His head turned and a low snarl escaped him when he heard the sound of running footsteps coming from both the direction of the cell and from the right corridor.

Rising, he removed the weapons from the other guards before darting toward the door. He hoped that Jordan had been successful at opening it. A sick knot formed in his stomach at the thought of her being unsuccessful. If she couldn't... his mind shied away from what would happen to her if Kelman captured her.

"Never," Dagger muttered under his breath.

Relief flooded him when he saw Jordan standing in the opened doorway, the tablet clutched to her chest and worry on her face. The sound of shouts behind him had him putting on a burst of speed. He exploded through the door at the same time as multiple laser fire erupted behind him. He turned as the door shut and the red light flashed to show that it was sealed.

Breathing heavily, he glanced over to where Jordan was turning to face him. A look of triumph crossed his face. The doors were blast-proof. The last thing anyone wanted was a spaceship exploding and taking half of the Spaceport with it.

"Let's go," Dagger said, turning back toward the *Lexamus IV*. "We need to leave now before they can intercept us."

Dagger glanced over his shoulder when Jordan didn't respond. She was staring at him with large, bright eyes filled with shock and... pain. His eyes swept down to where she was holding out one hand. It was covered in blood. The blood that was slowly spreading across the front of her shirt.

"Dagger," Jordan whispered, looking at him with pleading eyes.

As if in slow motion, the tablet she was holding fell from her other hand. Horror gripped him when she swayed a moment before her knees gave out on her. He rushed forward, catching her before she hit the floor. Lowering her to the ground, he brushed the hair that had caught on her lips back with a trembling hand.

"Jordan," Dagger choked, his eyes moving to the front of her scorched shirt. "You can't... I can't..."

Chapter 9

Dagger looked down through the clear cylinder of the medical unit at the peaceful features of Jordan's face for the hundredth time. His hands splayed across the glass, staring and willing her to live. Each moment she didn't wake was another moment that he felt like he was locked in a cell far darker than any he had been held in before.

"Warning, incoming vessels approaching," the computer system announced.

Dagger jerked back and turned. He had set the defense system to monitor any vessels tracking the same direction as the *Lexamus IV*. Glancing one last time at Jordan's pale features, he turned and headed for the bridge of the *Lexamus IV*.

"Activate defense systems," he ordered as he slid into the pilot's seat. "Show vessels."

"Defense systems activated," the computer responded. "Two Class C Star Ships are approaching at zero, eight, four, three point six clicks."

"Affirmative," Dagger responded, bringing up the manual controls.

His hands paused for a fraction of a second, his eyes flashing over the blood, Jordan's blood, that still stained them. For the past two days, they had been traveling through the far side of the star system, staying one step ahead of Kelman and his band of mercenary followers. He had barely had time to place Jordan in the on board medical unit, hook up the lifeline that would keep her alive, and seal her in a deep sleep in the stasis cylinder until he could properly look after her.

They were still too close to the Spaceport for him to take care of her wounds. She was stabilized for now in the medical unit, it was all he could do before he was forced to get them away from the Spaceport. Every chance he got, he returned to check on her to make sure that she was still stable.

He could still see Kelman's mocking face through the window as he picked up her limp body. Now, more than ever, he was determined to kill the mercenary. Taking defensive actions, he checked the coordinates of known planets in the star system. He needed to find a place to hide. While the *Lexamus IV* was state of the art and faster than most vessels, so were the ones Kelman was using.

He cursed when an alarm sounded. "Prepare for impact," the computer stated. "Rear shields set at maximum. Diverting power to shields."

"Do not divert power from the medical unit," Dagger ordered. "Confirm."

"Confirmed," the computer replied as a blast knocked him forward in his seat, triggering the automatic restraints in it. "Shields at eighty-four percent. Recommend diverting all unnecessary power to shields."

"Negative," Dagger retorted harshly. "Manual override. Load and lock rear laser cannons."

"Confirmed," the computer replied.

Grim determination filled him as he twisted and turned in an effort to avoid the impact of the blasts aimed at disabling the *Lexamus IV*. The one advantage he had over the other ships was the mobility of this one. It was small and sleek, made for moving quickly in and out of tight areas.

His eyes focused on a small cluster of asteroids. Even if he could get to them, they were still too far apart to provide any type of protection. Yet, if he could get close enough to one to destroy it, that was a different matter. Focusing on his target, he increased the speed of the *Lexamus IV*. The closest asteroid would come into view in a matter of minutes.

Another blast violently shook the *Lexamus IV* causing the lights to flicker. Dagger impatiently shut off the alarms and manually rerouted power to the shields. His eyes swept over the screen as the asteroid appeared.

"Warning," the computer said. "Imminent impact probable. Evasive maneuvers advised."

Dagger was well aware that there was a possibility of impact. He also knew that he needed to be close enough to shield the asteroid, destroy it, and get through the debris before the two ships gaining on him knew what he was doing. At this speed, the larger ships wouldn't be able to avoid it. The key was having the element of surprise so they could not avoid the debris field.

"Warning," the computer stated again.

Dagger's hand flashed to the controls and he shut it off. His hands tightened around the grips of the manual control navigation system. He slowly counted under his breath as he adjusted the front laser cannons.

"Ten, nine, eight, seven...." Dagger whispered under his breath, rocking again as another blast hit him. "Fire!" He ordered.

Twin blasts, intensified by his rerouting power from the rear cannons to the front, struck the Gartaian-sized asteroid. The super-heated bursts tore through the center of the asteroid, shattering the silicate and metal-ore into thousands of deadly missiles.

He twisted on the controls to the *Lexamus IV*, pulling to the side. Cursing loudly, he heard the outer hull striking the deadly debris. He had to lower the front shields to give him the additional power he needed. The maneuver left the *Lexamus IV* momentarily vulnerable. The two ships behind him weren't as mobile. The one closest to him could not react as quickly. He watched on the monitor as the outside of the ship's hull lit up.

Heavy pieces of the metal struck the *Lexamus IV*'s outer shields as they came online. Dagger redirected the power to the rear laser cannons and fired a volley of blasts. A sense of triumph coursed through him when the combination opened a rift in the attacking ship's shields, allowing the debris through. Unprotected, the thick pieces of metal-iron ore pelted the ship and ripped through the outer engines.

The ship behind him exploded. The force of the explosion, combined with the remains of the asteroid forced the second ship behind it to veer to avoid colliding with it. A swift scan showed that it appeared to have sustained damage from the explosion. Dagger hoped so as he pulled further away from the attacking vessels.

"Warning, engine one overheating. Emergency shut down and compartment sealing has been activated," the computer suddenly announced, pulling his eyes down to the readings being displayed.

Dagger cursed under his breath. The distance between the *Lexamus IV* and the other ship continued to grow, giving him hope that it was damaged too extensively to follow him. Checking the readings, he noted with relief that the fuel levels remained intact. He needed to find a safe place to land where he could check out the damage and hopefully repair it.

"Computer, open communications…," his voice died as he realized that he chanced giving away his location to Kelman or the Dreluthan. "Cancel. Computer, identify habitable bodies in this region."

"There are four worlds capable of sustaining life within reach of the current position," the computer replied.

"Show me each one," Dagger commanded.

His eyes flickered over the statistics for each one. The first two had large mining operations. He immediately eliminated them. In this region, if there were mining operations, they were more than likely populated by slavers and convicts. The third was a small moon that was covered by water, and while it could support life, it also had massive storms that would rip the *Lexamus IV* apart. The fourth was his only option. It was the smallest of the four and covered by thick vegetation and mountains. It was also the home of the Gartaians.

"Computer, plot course for the Gartaian planet," Dagger ordered.

"Confirmed," the computer replied. "Destination has been set."

"System status," Dagger asked in a rough voice.

"Shields at seventy-two percent, engine one currently offline, weapons system at twenty-four percent, hull integrity intact, environmental and medical within normal operational status," it responded.

"Monitor for any incoming vessels," Dagger ordered, releasing the straps that had automatically extended and wrapped around his chest when the first blast struck the *Lexamus IV*. "Maximum range."

"Confirm," the computer replied.

Dagger wearily swiveled the chair around and rose. Running a hand through his short hair, he pushed back his exhaustion. He needed to make sure that Jordan was still stable and set up the surgical tube. He didn't have time before, but he would now. The longer he waited, the less chance she had of surviving. The stasis chamber could only keep her alive for so long.

The thought that she might already be lost to him drove him down the narrow corridor. The *Lexamus IV* had three levels to it. The top section which contained the bridge and weapons systems. The second, which contained the medical unit and the living and dining areas, and the third level, which held the engine room and cargo area.

Whoever owned the ship before Arindoss had set it up with an advanced computer system so it could be operated by just one person. Dagger stepped into the lift and gave the command for the second level. He quickly squeezed through the doors before they opened all the way.

Jogging down the corridor, he turned into the open door of the medical unit. His eyes immediately went to the readings above it and he breathed a sigh of relief when he saw that the lights all showed normal.

Slowing his pace, he walked over to the stasis unit. His eyes softened as he stared down into Jordan's face again. The expression in them turned dark, menacing when he noticed the splatter of blood along one cheek. His eyes moved down and a low, burning fury scorched through him at the sight of the bruising along her neck. The vivid imprint of fingerprints showed clearly against her pale skin.

His mind fought to remember if he had been the one to hurt her. A part of him shied away from the knowledge that he could have hurt her and not remembered it. His gaze swept down to her wrists. The sleeves of the cloak still draped around her slender figure. They had pulled up and he grimaced when he saw the bruises around each fragile wrist.

Regret seared through him as he realized that he remembered grabbing her when she came into his cell. His stomach rolled at how close he came to killing her. Just the thought of it made him bend over the clear tube and draw in a deep, calming breath in an attempt to regain control of the emotions threatening to suffocate him. Reaching up, he pressed the control to start the process of bringing Jordan out of the stasis unit.

He would need to work fast. Turning, he pulled the cylinder for the surgical unit out of the wall. Within minutes, he had it ready for her. He turned when the stasis unit chimed to let him know that it was safe to remove her from it. His eyes went to the monitor when an alarm sounded.

"Don't," he ordered huskily when he saw the drop in her vital signs. "Don't you dare die on me, Jordan Sampson. I… just don't."

Dagger gently lifted her body in his arms and turned toward the other narrow bed. Laying her on it, he reached for the sharp pair of scissors in the tray that pulled out with it. He quickly cut off the cloak, her shirt and pants. Sliding his hand under her calf, he carefully pulled her boots off.

He couldn't prevent his gaze from returning to the wound on her right side. The skin was dark and blistered. Dried blood mixed with fresh where he had pulled her shirt away from the wound and it had been stuck to her skin.

"Please," he whispered, touching her cheek with trembling fingers even as his other hand pressed the control to close the lid. He didn't pull away until he had no choice. "Live… for me."

He watched as the lights from the scanner moved over her. His eyes briefly closed as the automated system took over. Twin arms detached and an injector attached to each arm pressed against either side of her bruised neck. The cylinder swept over her body, the band pausing over the damage to her side. He blindly moved over to a chair set against the wall and sank down into it. Blinking rapidly to clear the burning in them, his eyes focused on the readings showing Jordan's vital signs. His mind drifted back to the first time they met.

* * *

Earth: Over Two and a half years before.

Dagger reached down and gently lifted the shivering body of the human female in his arms. "You are called Jordan?" He remembered asking in a husky voice.

He would never forget her beautiful eyes as she turned to look up at him. They were filled with tears of pain, even though he was doing everything he could to be gentle. Her body had been hot to the touch despite the frigid air. He had drawn her as close to his body as he could without hurting her more.

"Why are you doing this?" Jordan had whispered.

"I will answer you if you confirm your name," he had retorted in a teasing voice when her lower lip poked out in a stubborn pout even as another shiver wracked her body. "Please," he remembered adding after she was silent for several seconds.

Her body relaxed and she turned her face into his chest, burying her cold nose against it, until he worried if she would be able to breathe. It took a moment, but he heard her muffled words. When he didn't immediately respond, she turned her head and glared up at him with quiet, defiant eyes.

"I said Jordan Sampson," she muttered. "My name is Jordan Sampson."

An amused grin curved Dagger's lips. It felt strange, as he wasn't the kind that 'grinned' very often. It was just the flash of defiance in her eyes and the beautiful pout to her lower lip when she was in no shape to defy him that he found… fascinating.

"I am called Dagger," he responded.

"Dagger what?" She asked, rubbing her cheek against his chest before releasing a sigh. "You feel so warm. I can't remember the last time I felt warm… or safe."

Dagger had to force himself not to tighten his grip around her as the soft, almost inaudible admission, escaped her. A strange, unfamiliar emotion coursed through his body again. There was a tightening in his chest, as if someone was squeezing his heart.

"I would keep you warm forever," he replied in a husky voice.

It took a moment for him to realize that the words had come from his mouth. Since when in the hell did he say mushy stuff like that… never! Shaking his head, he scowled at Saber, who was looking at him with a strange expression before he grunted when the female he was holding kicked him in the shin again.

"Will you stop that!" Saber snapped. "We are trying to help you."

"Well, keep your dirty paws to yourself and off me!" The girl retorted with a glare.

"I should just tie you up and haul your ass out of here," Saber growled in a low, menacing voice guaranteed to make anyone think twice about riling him, anyone it would appear except for the tiny blonde haired female glaring back at him.

"I can run circles around a big ape like you," the girl scoffed. "You'd never catch me."

"Taylor," Jordan whispered, turning her head to wearily stare at her younger sister. "Jesse!"

Dagger saw where Jordan's pain-filled eyes were focused. Hunter had returned with the body of the female they had originally been searching for. His friend's face was set in a fierce mask of determination.

For the first time, Dagger could understand and appreciate what Hunter must have been feeling as they searched for the human named Jesse. There was something about the females that pulled at the protectiveness in them… Well, except for Saber, who was cursing. The tiny female he was holding had sunk her teeth into his arm again. The moment he opened his hand, she had slipped away to hover near Hunter.

"Does she live?" Saber asked, rubbing his arm.

"Yes, but she needs medical attention," Hunter replied in a low voice. "Call for a transport."

"Already done. I'll see how far out they are," Saber replied before speaking quietly into the comlink attached to his ear.

"They're going to be okay, aren't they?" Taylor's worried voice asked. She turned to look back and forth between the three men before her eyes locked with Saber's. "You can help them, can't you? I… Jesse and Jordan are all I have. Please, you can make them better, can't you?"

Dagger watched as Taylor's eyes filled with tears. Shifting his gaze to Saber, he bit back a chuckle. Saber's face was filled with a panicked, almost desperate look, as he glanced back and forth between her sisters, before finally locking again on Taylor's pleading eyes.

* * *

Dagger muttered another apology under his breath as he climbed up the slanted slab of concrete. Jordan knew her low cry of pain was probably echoing in his ear. A sigh of relief escaped him when they reached the top and he straightened up. Her eyes flashed with fear when she saw an alien transport sitting almost a hundred yards away, nestled between two ruined buildings.

"You don't have to apologize," Jordan whispered, laying her head wearily on his shoulder. "It's not your fault I hurt."

Dagger's grunt was his only reply to her as he began walking toward the back of the transport. The never-ending rain had begun again, this time a little harder than before. Jordan watched as he nodded to one of the warriors that was waiting at the end of the platform.

"How bad?" The man asked, glancing at her pale face.

"Bad enough," Dagger replied in a grim voice.

Jordan closed her eyes and shivered, she didn't understand what they were saying, but she knew it had to be about her from the looks they exchanged. She was so tired, not just physically, but mentally.

She knew she must look like a drowned rat and she felt worse than a week old roadkill. She just hoped she didn't smell like it. Daily baths had become a dream of the past.

Instead, she, Taylor, and Jesse made do with rain water, heated, if they could afford the luxury. They used scraps of material as a washcloth, and the few precious bars of soap they had managed to steal from different abandoned homes, hotels, and stores over the last four years was almost gone to and it was becoming harder and harder to find anything left behind anymore.

The best thing about living here was that water was plentiful and the weather mild to freezing so she didn't have to worry about sweating that often. The bad part about living here was everything was dirty.

Jordan gazed around at the interior of the 'spaceship'. While it might not be one that went into space, it still flew like the ones in the movies and was the closest thing to something out of this world that she had ever seen. The interior was lit with red lights. She knew they probably did that to preserve their night vision, but it made the interior feel even more out of this world.

Her arms tightened around Dagger's neck when he started to set her down on a long, flat bed. Her heart started pounding, making her already beaten and battered body hurt even more. Tears silently slid down her cheeks and the shivering from the cold, fever, and shock increased until her teeth were chattering.

"Please, don't let me go," she whimpered. "Not yet. I... Please, I can't... not yet."

Dagger glanced at the man standing near the cot and shook his head. "Take care of the other one first," he ordered in a low voice.

Relief filled her when Dagger moved to one of the bench seats instead and sat down. Her arms loosened and she pulled them down, trying to get closer to his warmth. Her teeth continued to chatter until she felt like one of those dancing teeth that you wind up and let go.

"I... I'm... sorry," she stuttered. "I... I'm just so cold and I..."

She turned her face into his chest as her throat tightened with tears to the point she couldn't talk anymore. She felt so defeated. How could life become so hard that she wasn't sure she could go on?

"Hush," Dagger whispered, brushing a hand along her hair. "Tell me what happened to you."

A shudder coursed through her body and she stiffened for a moment before she relaxed. What did it matter anymore? She had no idea of what would happen to them now. Hell, she didn't even know what the Trivator warriors did to their prisoners. At least they were trying to help them other than….

"I was attacked," she forced out, closing her eyes. "The other night, Jesse and I were looking for food. We haven't eaten in forever. I didn't realize that Jesse had stopped. I was so excited to get back to Taylor and show her that we had found some food. The alley…" Her voiced died and she knew she was crying again. "There was an alley that we were cutting through, a shortcut. I didn't see the man in it. He attacked me. He… he kept hitting me, over and over, then he fell on top of me. I could feel my ribs hurting when he hit me, but when he fell on top of me, I heard a snap. I tried to scream, but he…"

Choking sobs escaped her and she turned her face into his chest again as the memories of that night just a few days before washed through her. She wanted to forget what happened. She wanted to wake up from the nightmare and think of it as a bad dream. Her dad would be calling to make sure she was home and ask if she had done her homework. Taylor would be excited about her next gymnastic competition, and Jesse would be humming under her breath as she cooked dinner.

"How did you escape?" Dagger asked in a low voice, careful to keep the anger in it hidden, less she thought it was directed at her.

"Jesse," Jordan replied, opening her eyes and staring up into his intense yellow-gold ones. "She heard me scream when he attacked. She killed him.

She saved my life and helped me get back to the parking garage, but…"

"But," Dagger encouraged, when she fell silent again.

Jordan's eye shifted to where Jesse was lying peacefully on the cot across from her. The Trivator called Hunter was sitting beside Jesse, gently stroking her older sister's hair while the other man that had greeted them checked Jesse. Jordan assumed the guy was some kind of a medic since he was checking Jesse like a paramedic or doctor would. Her eyes flickered to where Taylor was sitting, watching everything with wide-eyes.

"She had to leave the food behind," Jordan finally finished. "It was too dangerous to go back and get it. We didn't know who else might have heard what was going on. Jesse might be able to fight off one man, but not two or more. What are you going to do to us?"

Dagger glanced at Hunter. His friend shook his head in warning. Whatever was going to happen, Hunter wasn't ready to share it yet.

"We will take you to our compound where our healer will care for you," he responded. "Then, you will be fed."

Jordan gazed up at him, unaware that suspicion and uncertainty shimmered in her hazel eyes for a moment before resignation filled them as she stared up at him. Her lips finally lifted at the corner in a rueful smile. Her eyes lighting with the first hint of amusement.

"If you throw in a long, and I mean a really long, hot shower with the healing and food, I just might love you forever," Jordan finally whispered before her eyes widened in surprise when she felt the press of cold metal against the skin of her neck.

"She needs rest," the medic informed Dagger. "The scans show she is running a higher than normal temperature. I also didn't like some of the other readings. She has to be in intense pain."

Dagger nodded, glancing down at Jordan when her head fell back against his shoulder. She frowned and blinked before her eyelids fluttered close and she sank into the peaceful darkness.

Bowing his head, he breathed in the rain fresh scent of her skin. "I will keep you to that vow," he whispered so softly that he knew no one else would be able to hear him. "You are destined to be mine, Jordan Sampson."

Chapter 10

Dagger jerked, unaware that he had fallen into a light, exhausted sleep. It took a moment for his mind to clear and for him to realize it was the soft chime of the surgery unit finishing that had woken him. He rose stiffly out of the chair and walked over to the unit.

He reached over and pressed the panel, opening the cover. His eyes flashed briefly to the readings above the unit, all signs showing normal. He breathed a sigh of relief as he turned his attention back to Jordan. Her cheeks were flushed with the slight pink color that he remembered.

His gaze moved down to her stomach. It was healed with only a faint red line showing where the skin had been torn and blistered. She would always carry a light scar from her wound, but at least she would live. He carefully picked up her arm and checked it as well. The skin was slightly pinker than the rest where it had been blistered, but would probably heal without a scar.

He started when she moved her arm until she was joining her fingers with his. He blinked several times, his fingers instinctively curling around hers. She was looking up at him with a silent, searching gaze.

"Did we get away?" She finally asked in a quiet voice.

Dagger drew in a deep breath before he could answer her. He nodded while he tried to regain control over his emotions. Turning, he sat down on the edge of the surgical unit and pulled her hand up to his lips. Pressing a hard kiss to her knuckles, he closed his eyes, willing the thickness in his throat to dissolve.

"Yes," he finally said, opening his eyes to stare down at her. "Yes, for now. We aren't out of danger yet."

"But, we are for now," she repeated with a sigh.

He watched as she turned her head with a frown and gazed around before looking down. A rosy blush rose over her cheeks when she realized that the only thing covering her were her bra and panties. Luckily, both were black and covered her as much as a swim suit back home would have. Still, she wasn't at the beach, but alone with Dagger.

"What happened?" She asked, looking back up at him. "I remember being shot."

"Yes," he snorted in a disgruntled voice. "I told you to seal the door."

A hint of a smile curved Jordan's lips. "I did," she replied. "After you were through. I just didn't do it fast enough."

The corner of his lip turned down and his expression grew dark as he stared down at her. "You almost died," he pointed out.

Jordan raised her fingers and touched the firm line of his lips. She couldn't resist rubbing her thumb along it as her own gaze turned haunted by the memories of watching him fight. What she had gone through was nothing compared to what he had endured for over two years.

"So did you," she whispered. "When I saw you fighting that creature…"

··*

Dagger pulled away from her and stood with his back to her. He curled his hands into a fist, trying to resist the urge to either shake her, or wrap his arms around her and never let her go. The urge to shake her came from the knowledge that he hadn't been crazy. He hadn't just imagined that she was there. She had been.

"Do you have any idea how dangerous that crazy stunt of yours was?" He asked harshly, refusing to turn around.

He didn't want her to realize that it wasn't anger he felt, but fear. Fear of what would have happened if Kelman or a hundred other males on Bruttus would have gotten their hands on her. Death would have been a blessing compared to what could have happened to her.

"Yes, I do," Jordan said, her voice closer than he expected.

He turned to discover that she had risen off the bed. The thin, thermal blanket that had been on a lower tray next to the bed wrapped around her. She looked so beautiful, so fragile, and yet, there was a strength about her that he remembered seeing back on Earth.

"If Kelman had discovered you...." Dagger swallowed.

Jordan took a step closer to him. He stood stiffly when she leaned in close enough to rest her cheek against his chest and slide her right arm around his waist. A soft sigh escaped her, just as it had the first time he had held her. His arms slowly moved to wrap around her and he laid his cheek against the top of her head and released a sigh of his own.

"When is the last time you ate?" He asked in a gruff voice when he heard her stomach growl.

He lifted his chin when Jordan tilted her head back so that she could look up at him. Her eyes danced in amusement and she gave him a rueful smile. He loved the little half smile she always gave him. She knew it too.

"It's… been a while," she admitted. "I think I had a snack yesterday, or maybe it was the day before. I seem to have lost track of time with all the running around."

Dagger scowled down at her. "Come on," he said, wrapping her hand in his and turning toward the door. "There should be some clothing on board. We'll search the cabins. You can get cleaned up while I fix you some food. The cabins are next to the dining area."

"What about you?" Jordan asked in concern. "When is the last time you ate? Or slept? Or had a chance to clean up?"

Dagger glanced down at her and shrugged. "I'm a warrior, I'm used to such things," he replied in a low voice.

Jordan pulled him to a stop and forced him to look at her. "You are a living being," she said just as quietly. "When Dagger?"

Dagger knew from the determined thrust of her jaw, that Jordan wouldn't budge. They may not have had a lot of time together, but he had memorized everything about her that he could before he left on what was to have been his last mission. When Jordan made up her mind, few things could change it.

Lifting a hand, he brushed back her long hair before running his fingers down her flushed cheek. He would never get tired of the silky feel of her skin. The only thing that worried him was after everything he had been through, that it might not be safe for her to be close to him. He had felt something snap inside him. Something that he wasn't entirely sure that he had control over.

"Once you are taken care of, I will take care of my own needs," he stated instead of answering her. "Come. We have a few hours before we reach a place where we must land. The *Lexamus IV* incurred damage. I must try to repair it."

"Can't you call the men who came to help you, or Trig?" Jordan asked, following Dagger into a small room off the long corridor.

"No," Dagger replied, striding over to where the storage panels were. "It is too dangerous. I can't chance Kelman intercepting the communication and tracking the signal."

He opened several, pulling out clothing that looked huge. He threw some items over onto the bed, before pulling another panel open. Inside were several pieces of smaller, feminine clothing. It would appear Arindoss either didn't travel alone, or he had enjoyed bringing things to a female back on Bruttus. Dagger suspected it was both.

Jordan held up the black leather pants, vest and blouse. An amused grin curved her lips when she glanced at the matching set lying on the bed. It would appear that black was the 'in' color for pirates and warriors alike.

"We'll be twins," she chuckled, glancing back at Dagger. Her eyes softened as she stared up at him and the smile on her lips faded. "I missed you."

A low groan escaped Dagger at her words. Stepping forward, he pulled her into his arms and pressed his lips against hers. He didn't kiss her the way he wanted, he knew if he did that it would be impossible to stop. They were still in danger and he would not do anything that could jeopardize her safety.

"Get cleaned up," he ordered in a gruff tone. "I need to take care of my wounds and fix you something to eat. I'll get cleaned up in the other room and meet you in the dining area."

"What if they find us?" Jordan asked, worry darkening her voice.

"I have the computer set to alert me," he replied, picking up the clothes he had thrown on the bed. "It won't take me long."

"You could… You could stay… in here with me," she offered, glancing shyly down at the floor as a rosy blush spread up her neck.

"Jordan," Dagger murmured, waiting until she looked back up at him. "Don't tempt me. It… I am not the same as I was before. That isn't saying much, but… I'm not sure that it is even safe for you to be with me."

The stubborn expression settled over her face again, reminding him that there was more to her than met the eye. Inside him, the beast that he had become turned at the challenge in her eyes. He wanted her in a way that was different from before. Two years ago, the emotions inside him were protective. Now, the need to protect was still there, but so was something much darker, more primitive.

"I'm not the same as I was either, Dagger," Jordan replied, tilting her head and staring back at him. "Go get cleaned up and take care of your wounds. I'll see what there is to eat."

Dagger's throat worked up and down before he gave her a brief nod and turned and walked out of the door. There was something different about Jordan as well, he reluctantly admitted. Lost in thought, he walked into the cabin next door, refusing to think of how much he wanted to take Jordan up on her offer.

* * *

Twenty minutes later, Jordan watched as Dagger's nose wiggled as he sniffed the air when he walked into the dining area. Her eyes swept over him, unable to believe that he was really here. He was dressed in the dark clothing that he had found.

He and Arindoss must have been very similar in build because the dark shirt, vest, and pants looked like they were made for him. Her eyes went to his wrists where he had rolled the sleeves back. The cuts and bruises around them from where he had been chained were gone.

Satisfied that he had really taken care of his wounds, she turned back to pull his dinner out of the wall oven. She had found the ship's supplies to be well stocked. Arindoss not only kept the *Lexamus IV* prepared for a quick escape, he also kept it stocked with the finer things in life. She had discovered the dried food storage contained gourmet meals. A separate section contained a wide variety of what looked like expensive wines and liquor that were stored in a temperature controlled section off to the side of the food storage.

Even the clothes she was wearing felt different. The shirt felt like it was made from the finest silk from the way it slid across her skin. The pants she was wearing, while made from a leather of some type, were extremely soft and pliable. Perhaps if Arindoss had paid a little more attention to who he hired, than to what he bought, he might have still been alive.

"That smells good," Dagger admitted, walking toward the table where she was setting a steaming plate of food on it. His mouth watered at the delicious smells. "I can't remember the last time I had a decent meal. I think it was when you and I…"

Jordan glanced up when his voice faded. An understanding smile curved her lips. There was nothing they could do about the past, she had learned that lesson early in life. What they did with the future was what mattered.

"I know," she replied. "You should see some of the food Arindoss has on board, not to mention the liquor. I swear, he must have been planning one heck of a party."

She turned away to retrieve her plate from the 'oven'. It was strange how she could take a package that looked like a pile of hard rocks, pop it inside the machine on the wall, and out came a meal that looked like the finest chef in the most expensive restaurant back in Seattle had just prepared it.

She turned back toward the table, pausing when she saw that Dagger's eyes had been on her and not the food in front of him. Warmth surged through her at the knowledge that he wasn't immune to her.

Doubt had threatened to overwhelm her when she was showering and dressing. The fear that he had decided that he didn't want or need her had sent a shaft of pain through her before she pushed it away. He had said he was worried it wasn't safe for her to be near him, not that he didn't want her.

They had both changed a lot over the last two years. She had been foolish to suggest that he shower with her. She should have been more concerned with his welfare than her own desires.

Swallowing, she continued to the table and slid into the seat across from him. They ate in silence for several long minutes before she looked up when he suddenly rose out of his seat. He crossed over to the storage panels, opened one, and pulled out two containers of water and returned.

"Sorry, I should have thought about something to wash it down with," Jordan said with a self-conscious laugh. "I was so distracted by the smell of the food and my stomach demanding I shovel it in, that all I wanted to do was eat."

A low, rough chuckle escaped Dagger. "Mine, too," he admitted. "Arindoss had good taste."

"Yeah, he did," Jordan replied, stirring the mixture of vegetables on her plate with her fork. "What happened after I... How did you get away? How did the ship get damaged? How are you going to fix it? Where are we going? What are we....?"

Her voice died when she saw the bemused expression on Dagger's face at all the questions she was throwing at him at once. He was staring at her with an intensity that made her flush and she nervously tucked her hair back behind her ear. Looking down at her plate, she took a bite of her food to keep her mouth busy.

"It has been so long since I've had a conversation," he replied in a quiet, reflective voice. "I thought about you, dreamed about you, while I was imprisoned. You were the only hope that I had. Your face, the memory of your voice, is what kept me going."

Jordan's eyes had risen at his first quietly spoken sentence. She lowered the fork in her hand to the table and rose out of her seat, unable to keep the distance between them. Walking around the table, she slid into his open arms when he pushed his chair back. Curling up against him, she wrapped her arms tightly around him.

"You weren't the only one," she admitted. "When they told me you were dead, I felt like a part of me had died as well. I couldn't lose you, too. The first week was horrible. I couldn't... I couldn't think. I couldn't feel anything, but pain and grief."

"How did you find me?" Dagger asked, running one of his hands down along her back while the other held her against his body.

Jordan's arms tightened around him, holding him like she would never let him go. She understood what Jesse had felt when Hunter had been captured. Jesse's determination to go after Hunter when she found out where he was, had been a driving force for her.

"I could still feel you in my heart," Jordan explained, not moving. "I snuck into Hunter's office when he left to go to the city a week later. He had forgotten to shut down the console he used in his office. I uploaded a software program I was designing. With a few tweaks, I was able to access the data he had on the attack. While two bodies had been found in the wreckage, there was no proof that the bodies belonged to you or Edge. The more I dug, the more I found. There were missing pieces in the investigation. Most of it was due to the fighting going on. The area was still hostile, and the team sent in had very limited time. There were two badly burned bodies, so they assumed it was you and Edge."

Chapter 11

Dagger's hand froze as she told him about what had transpired. He remembered very little. He vaguely recalled the missile that struck their fighter. Fragmented images of them crashing in the city filled his head. They had skimmed the tops of several buildings. The wings of the fighter had been ripped off and they had crashed in a small courtyard area of the city.

He didn't know how they survived. Edge had been unconscious. Dagger knew he had suffered a concussion. The strong smell of fuel had forced him into action. He had unstrapped and kicked open the side door of the transport. It was the only exit accessible to them as part of the building had collapsed on the back of the fighter.

He vaguely remembered checking to see if Edge was alive and unstrapping the warrior. It had been a struggle, but he had half carried, half dragged Edge out of the fighter and dropped his body under a section of roof that had been destroyed from a nearby building.

He had turned to go back to the fighter to retrieve weapons and supplies when he saw two rebels crawling into it. Seconds later, there had been a tremendous explosion. He had been thrown backwards, striking his head again. The next time he woke, he was on a rebel transport in a cage. The next two years, he had literally fought to stay alive in the hopes of finding a way to escape. He had no idea that his people thought he was dead.

"Edge?" Dagger asked in a husky voice.

He felt Jordan shake her head. "Nothing yet," she said with a sigh. "I've been searching, but not like I have for you. I did tell Hunter that I believed he was alive as well. There has been an intense search, especially once they realized that I was right about you. I kept following leads from what they knew of the mercenaries that had attacked the planet. Everything kept leading to Kelman. I had a terrible time finding him. He is very good about covering his tracks."

Dagger's hand started moving on her back again. He felt her sigh as she rubbed her cheek along the trace of warm skin that was revealed by the open neck of his shirt. A heavy wave of need flooded him. It had been over two years since he had been with a female. Hell, he hadn't touched another woman since he met Jordan.

During his captivity, the need for survival was paramount to everything. Kelman knew he would either use or kill anyone placed in the same cell with him. Kelman and the guards had taunted him a few times, but soon bored when he showed no interest.

Now, his body woke with a vengeance. He wanted Jordan with a primitive need that made sweat bead on his brow. Dagger drew in a deep breath, trying to calm the fire burning inside him. The flame that had simmered for two years burst into a roaring inferno when Jordan shifted her left hand up and ran her fingers up the open neck and along his skin.

"Jordan," Dagger choked in a voice laden with need. "It is dangerous. I want... need you."

He felt her shift as she sat up on his lap so that she could look at him. Her eyes were darker and a small, secretive smile curved her lips before she leaned into him. Her left hand curved around his neck even as her right hand moved to touch the side of his face. She paused a breath away from his mouth.

"I need you, too," she whispered before pressing her lips to his in a shy kiss that quickly turned to hot need.

The slender thread that Dagger had desperately been trying to hold onto snapped when Jordan's right hand rose to splay across the back of his head and her lips parted. His arms tightened around her, moving so that he could lift her. Breaking the kiss, he rose out of his seat, their unfinished dinner forgotten as he strode from the room and into the cabin next to the dining area.

"You are my *Amate*, Jordan Sampson," Dagger gritted as he lay her down on the bed. "Mine for always."

Jordan searched his eyes as he pulled back to unfasten his vest and pull it and his shirt off. She watched, mesmerized. He bent and pulled off his boots before standing straight, his hands on the waistband of the black pants he was wearing. Her heart pounded with anticipation as her eyes followed the movement.

"What about...?" Her voice died as his fingers flick the top fastening of his pants and she swallowed.

"The computer will warn if any ships approach," he informed her in a rough voice. "We have at least two more hours before we reach the planet where we can land. It is too dangerous to continue with just one engine."

Jordan just nodded. She heard the slight warning in his voice and understood what he was not saying out loud. This might be the only time they have together. If Dagger didn't fix the engine, they could be left vulnerable to Kelman or any other pirate ship.

It was safer to land and try to do the repairs than to hobble along on one engine in space. If it couldn't be repaired, they stood a better chance of surviving on the planet where they could send out a signal and hide until help could arrive. Either option held the potential to end badly for them.

She pulled in a deep breath when he leaned down and cupped the calf of her left leg. He paused, his eyes locked with hers. The burning intensity in them took her breath away. She relaxed, lifting her leg so he could remove her boot. She did the same with her other leg.

"Dagger," she whispered in a husky voice when he leaned over her and began unfastening her vest, then her blouse. "My *Amate*. I am Jordan. I belong to Dagger as he belongs to me. Forever will I tie my life to his. I will care for, protect and cherish him as he cherishes me. He is my *Amate*. He is… my entire life," she whispered, lifting her hand to touch the ragged scar on the right side of his face that would always be a part of him.

Jordan felt the cold air brush across her bare breasts as he pushed the vest and blouse she was wearing open. She hadn't put her bra back on in her hurry to make sure Dagger was still there. Her hands frantically moved over his bare shoulders when he shifted so he was above her and sealed his lips to hers. She lifted her hips far enough for him to push her pants down with one hand, then the other. She was only vaguely aware of them sliding down the rest of her leg and her pushing them off the end of the bed.

Heat exploded low in her belly when she felt his hot flesh pressed against hers. Skin against skin, hard against soft, was an aphrodisiac to her system. An intense spear of desire pierced her, causing warm moisture to pool low between her thighs. Pleasure exploded through her at the thought of finally becoming one with the man she had fallen in love with on a night that seemed so very long ago.

..*

Dagger's hands shook as Jordan's softly spoken claim washed over him. The fact that she was claiming him, telling him in the words of his people that he belonged to her, stunned him. He hadn't been prepared for not only her acceptance of him, but her own determination to seal her life to his without question.

The beast inside him roared in triumph, wanting to accept her claim and more. His whole body was taut and hard with anticipation. He felt the pressure building in his sack until he was afraid he might explode. His cock, full and straining, pulsed against the inside of her thigh. He wanted to join with her, but knew she needed to be ready. Lifting his head, he gazed down at her.

"Jordan, my beautiful *Amate,*" he groaned, tangling his hands in her hair and pressing his lips to hers.

She opened for him, kissing him back with a passion that washed over him in crashing waves, taking away the anger and hatred and replacing it with peace and hope. His tongue tangled with hers, brushing against the smooth edges of her teeth. He groaned again when he felt her delicate hands skimming over his side and back. It felt like she was trying to memorize the feel of him against her.

Breaking the kiss, he rolled on the bed, taking her with him so that she was on top and in control. He needed to let her set the pace, even if it practically killed him. His hands spanned her waist, holding her slightly up off of his body.

Her hair fell forward, cocooning them as she gazed down at him. His eyes burned when she ran her gaze over his short hair. She reached out and touched the closely cropped strands. A smile played around her mouth.

"I like it," she said, looking back into his eyes. "Long or short, it doesn't matter, but it must be easier to take care of."

A low chuckle escaped him. "Only you would see the bright side of my hair being cut at a time like this," he retorted in a teasing voice. "I want you so badly that I am ready to explode."

Jordan's eyes glittered with mischief and she leaned down and brushed a kiss on the top of his nose before she teased his mouth. She pulled back just far enough that he could feel her breath against them. His hands moved around to cup her ass and he gently massaged the rounded cheeks.

"I want to explore you," she whispered against his lips. "I want to memorize every inch of you. I dreamed of this day, Dagger. From the moment you told me that I was yours back on the *Star Raider*, I've dreamed of being yours in every way. I don't want either of us to forget tonight."

Dagger's eyes softened when she pulled back to look at him with slightly pleading eyes. He saw how much she meant what she was saying. He also understood that she was doing this as much for him as she was for herself.

He lifted his hand and touched her smooth cheek. She turned her face into his palm pressing a kiss to it before swiping the center with the tip of her tongue. Her eyes danced when a low vibration of desire escaped him. Heat scorched him and he knew going slow was going to be the hardest battle he had ever fought.

"As long as it goes both ways," he replied, lifting his hands to cup her breasts. Her face flushed with pleasure when he rolled her taut nipples between his fingers. "Just… don't take too long to discover me."

He saw her head nod in agreement even as she relaxed back against him. Focusing his attention on her breasts, he rose up into a half sitting position and captured one of them between his lips. Her arms instinctively curled around his head, pulling him closer.

The heady scent of her arousal told him of her pleasure. Rolling the tip of his tongue over it, he was rewarded with a low moan and the tightening of her thighs on each side of him. Her hips moved in rhythm with his sucking and her fingers curled into his scalp.

"Oh, Dagger," she moaned, throatily.

He ran his hands over her back from her shoulders down to her ass. Shifting, he turned again, unable to stand the rotation of her hips on him. Every time she moved backwards, the tip of his cock brushed against her ass. It took every ounce of self-discipline he had not to lift her and thrust upward.

Pressing her backwards on the bed, he continued to lavish his attention on her breasts. His body was thrumming with sexual tension as he knelt between her legs. He released the rosy peak that he had been sucking on so he could press a kiss under the heavy globe.

"I want you," she panted, shifting restlessly on the covers. "I… didn't realize that wanting someone could… almost hurt."

"It is a good pain," he promised, pressing a kiss to her stomach. "A very good pain."

* * *

Jordan wasn't sure if he was telling her the truth or not. She knew what happened between a man and a woman. Hell, she had lived in a gaming world for years where sexual innuendos had been rampant. Still, she hadn't expected such a physical reaction.

Her skin felt super sensitive. Every time he ran his rough palms over it, she felt like screaming for more. Her heart was beating faster and her breasts ached for his touch. When he had taken the first one into his mouth, something had burst inside her making her ache lower.

The panting that had started when he was stroking her breasts turned to deep gasping breaths when he moved down her stomach to the triangle of curls. Jordan felt like she was shattering when he touched her there for the first time. Her body bowed and she bit her bottom lip in an attempt to keep the loud cry from escaping her.

"Dagger!" She cried out hoarsely when he ran his finger over her damp curls before he opened her to his lips. "Oh!"

Nothing had prepared her for the barrage of emotion and feelings overwhelming her. Her legs fell open and her hips instinctively rose to meet the hot touch. Her hands kneaded the covers since she couldn't reach him.

She could feel the hot moisture pooling between her legs, making her slick to his touch. She felt wanton and ached for something more. The low throbbing that had started early was now a heavy pulse. Unsure of what exactly was happening to her, but unable and unwilling to stop him to find out, she closed her eyes and just let him continue the magic.

If this is what discovering each other meant, then she was more than willing to let him explore. A hiccup escaped her when she felt him begin to slide a finger into her. It felt foreign, but instead of making her uncomfortable, her body seemed to welcome the intrusion.

"Dagger," she moaned as he pressed forward

He intensified his attack on her clitoris, causing her to cry out at the same time as he pushed forward. Jordan felt a fleeting flash of pain, but the power of the orgasm that broke over her at the same time as he pushed through the thin barrier of her virginity swept it away before it registered. Her body pulsed as wave after wave of explosive pleasure burst through her.

A low, startled cry escaped her when he rose above her and gripped her hips in his large hands. She felt his cock align with her still pulsing core. He looked down at her as he pressed forward.

An intense expression, a combination of desire and pain, was frozen on his face as he pushed forward. She raised her legs to wrap around his hips and dug her heels into the upper curve of his ass. Her eyes locked with his as he pushed forward.

"Jordan, my *Amate*," he whispered in a rough voice. "You are mine forever."

Jordan's eyes brightened with moisture at the emotion on his face as he held himself still to give her body time to adjust to his claim. The intensity, warmth, and emotion in them showed her more than any words could that he loved her. She raised her arms to him, needing to hold him.

He bent forward, sliding his hands up her hips past her waist before wrapping them around her back and pulling her close to him as he began to rock back and forth. Her arms slid around him and her eyes closed. She wanted to forever lock this moment into her memories.

The warmth of his breath caressed her neck as his arms tightened around her. His hips moved in slow, precise strokes at first, but as his breathing increased, so did the power of each stroke. She could feel the pressure building inside her again.

A low moan escaped her and her fingers kneaded his skin, her hips rotating and moving in rhythm with him as she fought her way to the top of the mountain. She knew the moment she reached it. Her body, full and humming from Dagger's hot shaft inside her, wrapped him in a fist and pulsed around him as she came again with an intensity that left her gasping.

"Jordan!" Dagger's harsh hiss echoed in her ear as he drove deep into her and froze, his loud pants of breath pulling at her heart. "Oh, my beautiful Jordan."

* * *

Dagger shuddered as his body pulsed deep inside his *Amate*. Her sweet taste was still on his lips. When she had come, he knew that he wouldn't be able to hold back. The thought of her hands and her mouth on him would have sent him over the edge. It had been too long for him and tasting Jordan's ambrosia had been like water to a dying man. It had flooded through him, healing the wounds not visible to anyone else.

He wanted their first time to be about pleasure, not pain. That was why he had brought her to a peak before he pushed through the barrier that he had felt. The taste of her orgasm mixed with the blood of her innocence sent a powerful, primitive wave of desire through him. He had risen up and pressed into her.

What he had not expected was her to lock gazes with him in understanding and acceptance of the emotions driving him. He had pushed deep into her and she met him all the way. They were partners, the other half of each other. He was the savage to her gentle, the primitive to her dark to her light.

When she opened her arms to him, he knew that was where he belonged. The feel of her body, connected to his, sent spears of pleasure rocking through every nerve-ending until he felt like shards of electricity were bursting and pulsing in a web of overload. Each stroke pulled him deeper and deeper into her hot core until he felt like they were one.

Just when he thought he couldn't feel any more pleasure, she shattered around him in one pulsing wave after another. Her hot channel had gripped him in a tight fist, stroking and squeezing the smooth skin of his cock. He had exploded, pouring his seed into her in pulsing streams.

It took several minutes for him to realize that the dampness on the skin of her neck was not from sweat, but from him. Tears that he had not known he was capable of shedding silently dampened her skin. They were tears of hope, relief, and joy for being given a second chance.

"You are mine," he brokenly whispered. "I am Dagger. I belong to Jordan as she belongs to me. Forever will I tie my life to hers. I will care for, protect and give my seed only to her. She is my *Amate*. She is my life. I love you, Jordan. You make me whole when I never thought it possible. You gave me hope when I had nothing else to hold onto. You… You make me… complete."

Jordan's fingers ran tenderly through his short hair. He felt the soothing touch, knowing that she recognized how fragile a thread he held on his emotions. After several minutes, she turned her head enough to press a kiss against his shoulder.

"I want to explore you," she whispered. "I want to touch you and hold you and never, ever let you go."

Dagger pulled back. Leaning on one elbow, he brushed her hair back from her face. Now… Now, he might be able to handle it. The key word was might.

Chapter 12

Dagger gently brushed the tangle of hair away from Jordan's peaceful face. She had fallen into an exhausted sleep after their lovemaking. Unfortunately, he could only let her rest for a short time. They both needed to be ready for the landing. It would be dangerous with only one engine. Leaning over her, he brushed a tender kiss across her lips and leaned back to watch as she woke for the first time in his arms. The fear that he would hurt her had dissolved under her gentle touch. Whatever magic she held in her slender palms had calmed the beast inside of him and soothed his battered soul.

"Is it time?" Jordan asked sleepily, yawning and snuggling against the warmth of his body. "I could stay here forever."

"We are nearing the planet. I need to pilot us in and I want to make sure that you are strapped in," he replied, letting his fingers drift down to her bare shoulder. "I love you, Jordan. You are an extraordinary female."

He watched as her face softened and glowed at his words. "I love you, too," she whispered, rising up to press a kiss to his lips. "Let's do this."

He nodded, swallowing over the lump in his throat. Rolling out of the bed, he grabbed his pants off the floor. He jumped in surprise when he felt a light slap across his ass. He turned to look at Jordan with a raised eyebrow. She was grinning at him in appreciation.

"Sorry, couldn't resist," she laughed, dancing away from him when his eyes brightened at her teasing. "Dress, we don't have much time."

Dagger ran his eyes appreciatively over Jordan as she pulled on her own clothing. When he was with her, he felt… right, complete. Pulling on his boots, he held out his hand to her.

"It is going to be a dangerous entry. I'll have to use the thrusters to try to keep the ship level. I don't want it to spin out of control as we enter the orbit of the planet," Dagger explained as they stepped out of the room and headed down the hall to the lift.

Jordan squeezed his hand tightly in hers. "What do you need me to do?" She asked in a husky voice.

"First and foremost, stay safe for me," he replied, pulling her into his arms as the doors to the lift closed around them. He held her tight on the short ride up. "I will probably need your help with the controls. It will be difficult to try to control the thrusters and keep the ship on course."

"I can do it," Jordan said with a reassuring smile. "I was a gamer. I have great control when it comes to things like that."

Dagger chuckled and shook his head. "I don't know what a 'gamer' is, but something tells me you were the best," he said, turning as the doors opened.

He led her down the corridor and paused at the door to the small bridge so that they could see the planet they were approaching. Out of the front view screen, the small red, green, and white planet on which they would take temporary refuge loomed before them. Stepping forward, Dagger motioned for Jordan to sit in the right seat while he took the left.

"Computer, show topography of the projected path," he instructed, punching in the commands for the manual override.

Glancing at the screen, he found what he was looking for. There was a huge cave located several meters above the thick jungle below. It would be difficult, but not impossible to land the *Lexamus IV* in it. Landing there would provide shelter from the creatures below, from the intense heat, and from any scans.

"That is our target," he said, pointing to the holographic image. "It will be difficult, but not impossible."

His eyes flickered to Jordan when she released a delicate snort and rolled her eyes at him. An unexpected grin curved his lips upward. She had that look on her face again. The one that said she was on a mission.

"I've got it," she replied, grinning at him. "We can do this."

Dagger nodded and turned his focus back on the planet as it grew closer. He redirected power to the front shields as they began their descent into the outer layers of the planet's atmosphere. Flickering a quick glance at Jordan, he saw that she was focused on the map in front of her.

"When we return to Rathon, I want you to wear my Claiming mark," Dagger muttered in a low voice.

Jordan didn't turn her head, but he saw the smile on her face. "I wouldn't expect anything less," she retorted lightly. "I think things are about to heat up a bit."

Dagger turned his head back toward the front. His jaw locked in determination. The front shields glowed with the red flames of entry, but were holding. He sent a series of burst from the thruster when the ship began to violently rock and began to dangerously lean to the left.

Neither one of them talked. Dagger held the controls, his focus on the readings in front of him. The temperature in engine two was rising. Jordan was doing an excellent job of guiding them, allowing him to focus on keeping the *Lexamus IV* level and monitoring the readings.

The *Lexamus IV* shook and rocked. The sound of alarms exploded over the rattling of the equipment and the roar of the over taxed engine. Dagger reached up and silenced it.

"Warning, engine two temperature levels rising," the computer stated. "Shields at thirty-four percent. Port thrusters at fourteen percent."

"Yippee Ki-yay, Mother Computer. Tell us something we don't know," Jordan muttered under her breath.

"We're through," Dagger shouted, briefly glancing over at Jordan's pale face.

Jordan didn't turn to look at him, just gave him a brief, strained smile. His eyes swept down to where her hands gripped the navigation stick. Her hands were wrapped around them and he could tell she was fighting to retain control. He silenced the computer and turned off the alarms when the ship rocked again before his hand returned to the thruster control.

"Heading sixty-four degrees, nine minutes," Dagger commanded the computer.

"Confirmed," the computer replied. "Thrusters at nine percent."

"Dagger!" Jordan cried out when the *Lexamus IV* tilted crazily and began to spiral out of control.

"I'm cutting power to the left engine," Dagger shouted.

The moment he cut the engine, the *Lexamus IV* began to rapidly drop. Using just the thrusters, he corrected the roll with a series of bursts from both the right and left stabilizer. His eyes flickered down to the power grid. They were down to four percent on the left thruster.

"There it is," Jordan called in a husky voice.

Dagger saw the cave as well. It would be an impossible landing. His eyes turned to a break in the forest showing on the screen. A long, narrow cut appeared between the thick jungle. They were descending too quickly and too fast to make the cave. If he didn't find another landing, they would crash into the side of the red mountainside.

"Take over the thruster control," Dagger ordered. "Keep us as level as you can."

He didn't wait for Jordan to respond. He didn't have time. Switching the control of the thruster to her, he took over piloting the *Lexamus IV*.

"Steady," he murmured, more to himself than to Jordan, who was releasing small bursts from each thruster. "Steady."

The ship clipped the top of the mammoth trees before it glided over them and dropped even lower. Dagger pulled up the nose of the *Lexamus IV* and shouted for Jordan to give full thrust as he lowered the landing gear.

"Dagger," Jordan cried out in alarm when the left thruster died just feet from the ground and the *Lexamus IV* tilted.

The *Lexamus IV* lurched as Jordan changed the direction of the thruster to compensate as the *Lexamus IV* landed heavily just feet from a large river that had been shielded by the tall, red grass and thick forest. It took several long minutes before either one of them moved, both still amazed that they had landed in one piece.

"We did it," Jordan's soft, astonished whisper echoed through the cabin. "I… We did it."

Dagger turned to look at Jordan. She was staring with wide eyes out the front of the view screen. His pride in her soared when he saw that her hand was trembling when she reached up to push her hair back from her face. No matter what the challenge, she didn't back down, nor did she give up.

Releasing the strap that had automatically extended, he swiveled in his chair and rose. Taking the step closer to her chair, he bent and turned her chair toward him before releasing her restraints.

Taking her trembling hands in his, he pulled her up and into his arms.

"Yes, we did it. Together," Dagger murmured, as he realized that Jordan wasn't the only one shaking.

Chapter 13

Jordan pushed back the strand of hair that had fallen forward as she cleaned up the mess in the dining area. Dagger was doing a systems check for damage and determining what needed to be done for the repairs. It had only been an hour since they landed, but there was a lot that needed to be done.

She had left him to do what he knew best while she decided she needed a hot drink to calm her nerves. She knew that she was close to having a quiet breakdown and didn't want Dagger to see her when she did. It was her way of dealing with all the stress and changes. Whenever she felt things becoming overwhelming, she would find a nice quiet place to be alone. Sometimes she would cry, sometimes she would just think and let the events play out until she could file them away.

That is what she was doing now. Well, while she cleaned up the mess from their dinner last night. She had forgotten all about the remains of the dinner they had left on the table. It had gone flying during their descent to the planet. Spying another piece of vegetable under the table, she crawled under and picked it up. She dropped it on the tray with the rest of the items and wiped the floor.

Scooting backwards, she scooped up the trays and cups and stood. A slight smile curved her lips as she thought about the reason that they had left the food on the table. Last night had been not only incredible, but more than she could ever have imagined.

She walked over and deposited the items in the cleaning unit. It would dissolve all the food particles along with it. Her mind wandered back to Earth as she rinsed out the cloth she was using and walked back to the table and chairs to wipe them down. A sigh escaped her as her hand moved slowly over the smooth surfaces. So much had happened over the last few years, especially since she met Dagger.

* * *

Star Raider: **Over two and a half years before:**

Jordan walked along the corridor of the massive spaceship feeling overwhelmed by it. Heck, she was feeling overwhelmed by everything that had happened in the last few days. The fact that she, Jesse, and Taylor had woken on a spaceship racing through a star system would have stunned anyone... human.

She swallowed as she passed several of the huge Trivator warriors standing in the hallway talking. She shied away from them when they stopped talking and gave her an assessing look. Wrapping her arms around her waist, she hurried past them.

She was searching for a place where she could be alone to think, to try to deal with everything that had happened since she had woken up. She was sharing a room with Taylor, and while she desperately loved her little sister, she needed to be by herself. Taylor was currently in a bad mood after Saber, one of the Trivator warriors responsible for them being there, had chewed Taylor out a short time ago in the training room.

Jordan could understand her little sister's anger. She was feeling pretty angry herself right now. She just held it in. None of them had asked to be taken from Earth. Hunter, another Trivator warrior, had 'claimed' her older sister Jesse as his *Amate*. Jordan had found out last night that *Amate* meant he had claimed Jesse as his 'wife'.

"Oh!" Jordan cried out in surprise when she felt a hand touch her arm from behind. Swirling around, she paled when she saw it was the same Trivator male that had saved her not once, but twice, back on Earth. "You… you… startled me," she said, stumbling backwards and looking away from his intense stare.

"Where are you going? You should not walk around without an escort," Dagger growled.

Jordan bit her lip, refusing to look at the man that was the cause of many of her feelings of confusion. Instead, she shrugged and started to turn away from him, hoping that if she just ignored him, he would leave her alone like the other warriors did. A shiver of unease and anger burst through her when she felt his fingers wrap around her arm.

"Don't touch me," she hissed in a low tone.

She felt his fingers loosen and he released her, but there was a feeling of reluctance to the movement. It was almost as if he didn't want to let her go. Tears burned her eyes as another wave of confusion swept through her. She just wanted to be left alone!

"My apologies," he responded in a stiff voice. "I asked where you were going. I will escort you."

"I don't know," she reluctantly admitted in a voice that was barely audible. "I don't know anymore."

She lowered her head to hide her face as it crumbled and silent sobs shook her thin shoulders. If she thought she felt lost at any time during the four years since these aliens had first appeared and their world had dissolved into a nightmare, it was nothing to what she was feeling now.

She didn't fight it when strong arms swept her off her feet. Instead, she felt that same sense of being cocooned in warmth and safety as she had the last two times he had held her. The first time had been in the parking garage when Dagger, Hunter, and Saber had found them hiding.

The second time had been when a large group of human men had attacked her and her sisters in the downtown area of Seattle after they had escaped from the Trivator compound. They had been searching for a way out of the city. Dagger, Hunter, and Saber had come to her and her sisters' aid after they were surrounded. They would have died that day if not for the Trivator warriors. Dagger had lifted her in his arms and held her protectively against him after saving her life.

"Hush, little one," Dagger murmured.

Jordan didn't know where he was taking her. At this point, she didn't care anymore. She was like Taylor, she had just wanted to go home, but unlike her little sister, she didn't know where home was anymore.

"I feel so lost," she whispered in a low, resigned voice. "I don't know where to go or what to do."

The arms around her tightened, but the man carrying her didn't respond. Unable to do anything else, she laid her head against his shoulder. She kept her eyes diverted from the warriors that stepped to the side and stared at them as they passed them in the hallway.

After numerous twists and turns, Dagger paused outside of a room. The door slid open and he stepped through. A moment later, it closed behind him. Curious, Jordan lifted her head and gasped in surprise. The room was filled with plants, thousands of colorful plants of all different sizes and varieties. Along a back wall, she saw the top of a waterfall.

"It isn't real, but it looks like it is," he murmured in a soft voice.

"Are the... Are the plants?" Jordan asked, staring at the brightly colored blooms of one plant as Dagger slowly walked forward.

"Yes," he said, gently lowering her to her feet.

Jordan swallowed when she realized that while he had set her back on her feet, he hadn't released her. His left arm had slid down and his fingers threaded through hers in a firm grasp. Jordan's fingers instinctively curled in return when he took a slow step forward.

"When I need time alone, I come here," he said, reaching out with his other hand and touching one of the plants.

"You need time, too?" She asked in surprise, looking up at him with wide eyes.

He glanced down at her and smiled. "Yes," he replied in a simple statement filled with meaning. "Watch."

Jordan watched in awe as he stroked the leaves of one plant with almost solid black leaves. As he did, lines of brilliant green light began to run in tiny rivers creating rippling waves outward. It was one of the most amazing, beautiful things she had ever seen.

"Can I touch it?" She asked, looking up at him before gazing down at the plant.

"Here," he murmured, taking the hand he was holding tenderly in his, and reaching out until the tips of her fingers were barely touching the leaf. "You have to be very gentle."

Jordan smiled in delight as she carefully stroked the leaf. It was mesmerizing watching the colors running through it. It looked almost like….

"Fairy dust," she whispered.

The strong fingers holding her wrist had shifted. A shiver ran through her when she felt the thumb caressing the inside of her wrist. He must have felt the shiver and thought she was cold, because he moved closer, until the heat of his body was pressed along her back.

Jordan actually felt her pulse jump at the feel of him and the knowledge that she was caged between him and the plant. What surprised her was the fact that instead of feeling panicked by the thought, she actually felt... safe. There was something strange about her reaction to him. When she was around any of the other warriors, she felt a slight sense of panic and the desire to make herself as small and invisible as possible, but with Dagger it was different. With Dagger, she wanted him to see her, to notice that she was there, and to be near him.

"What is fairy dust?" He asked in curiosity, sliding his other hand around her waist and pulling her closer.

Jordan released a shaky breath and stilled her hand against the plant. Closing her eyes, she tried to remember why she shouldn't like this. He was an alien, after all. He, Hunter, and Saber had taken her and her sisters from their world. He had… saved her life and made her feel warm and safe.

"Fairies sprinkle it over things," she whispered. "Fairies are small creatures that are magical. They are known to live in the forests and take care of it. They can sprinkle their dust on things and wonderful things happen."

Her heart began to pound when he threaded his fingers through hers again and turned her to face him. She tilted her head back and looked up at him. Her lips parted slightly when he pulled her closer to his body with his other hand.

"I don't remember seeing any of these creatures while I was on your world," he replied with a frown. "I spent some time in the forests outside of your city."

"They aren't real," she explained with a shy laugh. "They are make-believe. Things that little girls dream of when they are young."

The frown cleared and he nodded. Jordan swore that his eyes were a darker yellow, almost gold, as he stared down at her. He was gazing down at her as if he wanted to say something, but wasn't sure. She saw a flash of frustration cross his face before he muttered an expletive in his language. A rosy blush swept up her cheeks when the translator embedded in her ear translated what he had said.

"I apologize," he said, releasing her and stepping back. "I should not have said that out loud."

"It's okay," she replied with a shy smile. "Jesse and I have been known to say a few similar things over the last couple of years. Even Taylor was on a rant just a little while ago."

She turned and started to walk down the narrow walkway that had been built to imitate a natural garden. Her fingers brushed along the plants as she walked. She could hear him following close behind her.

"Have any of the warriors approached you?" He asked.

Jordan glanced over her shoulder with a frown and shook her head. "No, why would you ask?" She said.

"I heard what your sister asked you," he replied, ducking under a thick red leaf as he followed behind her. "Have any of the other warriors made you feel threatened?"

Jordan paused for a brief moment, before she shook her head and continued forward. She gasped when he swung her around the moment they had reached the area in front of the waterfall. The path had ended and a short, yellow-type fern covered the area in front of it.

"Tell me the truth," he said. "If they have, I will deal with them."

Jordan looked up at him in confusion. His face had turned dark with a savage looking scowl, but for some reason, it still didn't scare her. Raising a hand to touch his cheek, she realized just how tall he was compared to her five and a half foot form.

"All the warriors have been very considerate," she swore, blushing and dropping her hand when his expression cleared. "She was just worried they were like…"

She turned away and stepped over onto the yellow fern. The memories of what had happened back on Earth threatened to choke her again. A part of her couldn't help but feel thankful that she was away from it. Fascinated by the illusion of the waterfall, complete with a light breeze and mist, she sank down to the ground and drew her legs up under her.

She glanced at Dagger when he lowered himself down beside her. Closing her eyes, a soft smile curved her lips. This place was just what she had needed.

A warm hand caressed her cheek. "The healer said the human males had not harmed you or your sisters in that way," Dagger replied in a gruff voice. "I asked." Jordan's face flamed and she would have pulled away if he had not moved his hand down to her chin. "He spoke the truth, did he not?"

"Yes, he spoke the truth," Jordan whispered. "You make me feel…. Strange inside."

A low groan escaped him and he pulled away. She watched as he rose to his feet and took several steps away from her. He kept his back to her, but she could both see and feel his frustration as he ran his hands through his long white hair. After several long seconds, he turned and looked down at her again.

"You are still young," he said in a voice that reflected his frustration. "It is not right. Hunter is your protector now. I… You are…."

Jordan rolled onto her hands and knees before standing up. She brushed her damp palms along the pants of the dark green tunic she was wearing. Licking her lips, she took a hesitant step toward him.

"I am… What?" She asked, stopping in front of him.

A wave of warmth and excitement rushed through her when he suddenly pulled her into his arms and held her tightly against his body. This time, she wrapped her arms shyly around his waist in returned. She felt the shudder that ran through him at her embrace.

"You are mine," he whispered.

* * *

Jordan's head jerked up when she heard the footsteps coming down the hallway. She blinked several times to bring her mind back to the present. She knew there was a silly grin on her face. There always was when she thought back to that time on the *Star Raider*.

Turning, the smile died when she saw the grim expression on Dagger's face. Biting her lip, she straightened and waited for him to tell her the bad news. He must have seen the expression on her face because his face relaxed and he opened his arms.

Jordan dropped the damp cloth onto the table and moved into his arms, wrapping hers around his waist and holding him tightly against her. It couldn't be all bad, she figured. They still had power.

"It isn't as bad as I suspected," Dagger assured her.

Jordan tilted her head back and looked at him with a narrow, assessing gaze. "If it isn't as bad as I think, then why the long face?" She asked.

Dagger released her and pulled back. He walked over to the same panel he had the night before and pulled out a container of water. Opening it, he took a long drink before wiping the sweat from his brow.

"There was a reason that I wanted to set down in the cave up in the mountain," he told her, reaching around to grab another drink out of the panel and bringing it over to her. He motioned for her to have a seat. "We are on a small planet in the Kepler-10 star system. We landed in a hammock area that is surrounded by a shallow river and swamp. The trees you see look like they are part of a forest, but most stand in several feet of water. There is a creature that lives here that is called the Gartaian."

"Isn't that what you fought?" Jordan asked, her eyes darkening with worry. "It was the huge gray creature, wasn't it?"

Dagger's lips compressed into a hard line and a look of disapproval lit in his eyes. "You were there longer than I realized. You shouldn't have seen such things," he muttered, glowering at her.

Jordan reached over and cupped his hand in hers, turning it over so that she could look at his palm. Faint scars and thick calluses lined it. She ran her fingertips over them as she contemplated how to respond to him.

"You asked me once how I found you," she finally replied in a quiet voice. "For two years I searched for you. I learned everything I could about the computer language that your people use. I met up with hackers online, and begged them to teach me everything that they could." A small, distant smile curved her lips as she thought of the endless hours she had spent learning and researching. "I guess there are some on every world. I found you several times, but by the time Trig or another team went after you, you were always gone. Each time they came back without you, I died a little more. This last time there was something that told me that I might not get another chance."

She looked up into his eyes, letting him see the tears shimmering in them. He reached up with his other hand and caught one that spilled over and slid down her cheek. She turned her face into his palm and pressed a kiss into it.

"Everyone else had given up on you, but I never did," she whispered. "I knew I had to come. If you slipped away, I would find you before they could take you too far. I slipped out of the house and went to your house. I knew that Trig was back. He was supposed to meet up with Hunter the next morning to give him a report. I had slipped out many times over the two years and gone to your house, hoping that you would be there, but you never were. Trig tried to force me to go home, but I refused. I told him that I knew where you were and that if he didn't take me, I would find someone who would."

"Jordan," Dagger said thickly, staring at her as she continued to explain how she had searched for him and what his disappearance meant to her.

"I can be very stubborn," she said, with a wry smile before it faded from her lips and her eyes hardened. "I started by finding out who was behind the attack on your fighter. I discovered it was led by a mercenary group, and Kelman's name came up. The problem was I kept running into a roadblock every time I tried to pinpoint his location. He moved frequently and even those in the underground groups wouldn't talk about him. I started tracking anyone that dealt with him, closing the circle until I finally found Arindoss. I knew that Kelman must be making a move to take over *The Hole*, either that, or he was planning on working with Arindoss. It was one of the largest fight rings outside of the Alliance's normal patrol zones."

"What you did was very dangerous," Dagger insisted, gripping her hand in his.

Jordan shook her head. "No more dangerous than spending four years on the streets of Seattle," she replied in a sad voice. "I learned a lot during that time. I'm better at blending into a crowd now. Some of my classmates gave me tips on that."

Dagger grimaced and released a savage snort. "Remind me to kill your classmates when we return to Rathon," he grunted, releasing her hand and picking up his drink.

Jordan chuckled and sat back. "The point I'm trying to make is I've seen a lot of bad things and lived," she replied in a quiet, steady voice. "It is not only the experience that we go through that make us stronger, but how we choose to deal with it. I choose to conquer my fears and to fight for what I believe in. I believe in you, Dagger. I told you that if you didn't come back, that I would come after you. I'll do it every time, no matter what."

"That appears to be a trait of the women in your family," Dagger replied in a gruff voice before he released a deep sigh. "I cannot change what has happened, or even what may be to come, but I will be beside you on the journey."

Jordan smiled. "I know," she said. "That is all I could ask for."

Dagger picked up his drink and finished it off. Setting the empty container on the table, he rolled it between his hands before he drew in a deep breath of resignation. She waited as he made up his mind whether to tell her what was bothering him.

"It is going to take me several days to repair the engine," he began before pausing again.

"But, that isn't what is bothering you," Jordan observed.

Dagger looked at her grimly and shook his head. "No, what bothers me is that we are in the open in the middle of the Gartaian feeding plain, the *Lexamus* is sinking into the soft soil, and we are vulnerable if Kelman or the Drethulan discover us before I can fix the engine."

"At least we are alive to do it," Jordan pointed out, leaning forward and cupping his hand again. "We'll fix it together."

Dagger looked at the delicate face across from him. Once again, he realized that Jordan was an amazing woman. She was young, and while she had already lived through so much, her spirit was as strong as any warrior that he had known and fought beside, including that of Hunter, Saber, and his brother, Trig.

"Have I told you that you are an amazing female?" Dagger murmured in a quiet voice.

Jordan chuckled and rose out of her seat. "You can show me once we get out of here," she teased.

Dagger rose as well, pulling her into his arms as she walked around the narrow table. He bent his head. He paused just a breath away from her lips, mesmerized by the look in her eyes. He saw the glimmer of love, hope, and belief shimmering back at him. They would get out of here. Pressing his lips to hers, the determination grew when her lips parted beneath his and she hungrily returned his kiss.

Chapter 14

They spent the rest of the afternoon working on the engine. Dagger glanced over at where Jordan sat on a rock in the shade of the Starship. She had a laser rifle in her hands and was continually scanning the area.

It helped having her guard while he worked. This way, he could stay focused. He wiped his forehead again as sweat ran down it. His eyes moved back to Jordan.

Her face was flushed from the heat and humidity and glistened with sweat, but she didn't complain. She had removed the vest and tied the shirt she was wearing at the waist. His eyes moved appreciatively to her bare legs. She had snorted and said that leather and heat did not mix. She had quickly returned with a pair of Arindoss' silk bed pants, rolled low at her waist and cut off.

"Dagger," Jordan quietly called out in warning. "I see movement."

Dagger set the torch he was using down and picked up the other rifle. He turned, his eyes scanning across the thick strand of trees from the shallow river. The area was flooded as well, but it would be no problem for the mammoth creatures to move through.

"Get on the ship," Dagger ordered when he realized that it was a large herd of the creatures.

"I'll cover you," Jordan replied in a soft voice. "Get the equipment, we can't lose it. They are almost blind, so if we stay in the shadows and get inside before they come across, we should be fine."

Dagger wanted to argue, but he knew that Jordan was right. They couldn't afford to lose any of the tools they needed for the repairs. Already the ship had sunk almost a foot into the soft ground. They would never get out if the landing gear sunk all the way. The four supports would act like an anchor, tying them to the ground.

He shouldered the rifle and quickly picked up the torches and other tools he had been using. The sun was beginning to sink into the horizon and dusk was upon them. That was when the creatures appeared to move out of the swampy forests and onto the drier land where the tall grass grew.

"Move," Dagger said as he watched a huge male Gartaian emerge out of the dark shadows. It paused in the middle of the river, as if sensing that it was not alone. "Now, Jordan."

Jordan nodded, keeping the butt of the rifle firmly pressed against her shoulder and her finger on the trigger. She turned when she heard a loud roar come from the opposite side. Her eyes darted back and forth when she realized that another male, this one younger from the light gray color of his skin, had come out of the opposing woods to her left.

"Uh-oh," she whispered, moving along the side of the Starship. "I think we are in the middle of a territory dispute."

"The younger male is challenging the bull," Dagger gritted out. "Get up the platform."

Jordan didn't argue. She twisted and climbed up onto the platform that they had left partially closed due to the Starship sinking. She reached down and grabbed the bag of tools that Dagger was holding up to her.

While the Gartaian were almost blind, they weren't completely. Dagger knew they could see the movement of shadowy figures. The biggest advantage they had was their sense of smell. It was excellent, just as he had discovered back on Bruttus. Fortunately, the two bulls were more interested in each other than in him and Jordan.

"Here," Jordan whispered, stretching out her hand to grab the last of the equipment while keeping an eye on the young bull as it pawed at the ground.

Dagger handed the small pouch up to Jordan before pulling himself up onto the ramp. He turned when he heard Jordan gasp. The old bull had accepted the challenge and had risen up onto his back legs. The loud sound of his bellows rung through the air before the two charged each other.

He didn't wait to see what happened. Slamming his hand on the door control, he sealed it just as the ground under them shook from the force of the two massive bodies colliding. Jordan was staring at him with wide eyes filled with emotion. From the expression on her face, he could tell that she was remembering the fight back on Bruttus.

He stepped forward and ran the back of his fingers down her flushed cheek. "I survived," he murmured. "I survived because I had something worth living for to come back to."

Jordan's eyes filled with tears, but they didn't fall. Instead, she gave a watery laugh. He loved that about her, that she could see past the pain.

"I didn't give you much choice," she teased. "I warned you what would happen if you didn't come back."

"Yes, you did," he murmured, his eyes darkening with emotion. "Let's get cleaned up."

He knew from the secretive smile on her lips, that she caught the meaning behind his words. He wanted to shower with her and then he was going to love her. Just the thought of holding her in his arms again stirred his body awake.

"I'll help you store the tools," she replied. "Then, we'll get cleaned up."

They worked as a team over the next half hour, recharging the torches and storing the equipment. His blood was boiling by the time they were done. Every time Jordan walked by him, she would brush her hand over him. It was just a soft touch across his ass, a finger down his chest, a flick across one of his nipples, or a blatant swipe across the front of his pants with a knowing look.

"Enough," he growled when she blew a warm breath along his neck as he bent to store the last of the materials. "You are a distraction."

He turned and scooped her up into his arms before she could dance away from him. She squealed when he pressed a wet kiss to her neck. The sound of her giggles washed through him, taking with it another layer of the pain and anger that had been his only companion for so long. It was music to a deaf man who suddenly discovered what it felt like to hear. Her dancing eyes, flushed face, and the happiness shining from it humbled him as nothing else could have. She gave with her whole heart.

"I love you, Dagger," she whispered, seeing the flash of vulnerability in his eyes again. "So very, very much."

His throat worked up and down and he nodded. Turning on his heel, he strode through the lower level of the ship to the lift. Stepping into it, he set her down, suddenly self-conscious of how dirty he was from working on the engine and that he probably didn't smell much better than the Gartaians outside.

"I need a shower," he said gruffly.

Jordan laughed again and nodded. "Yes, so do I," she giggled, wiping at a dark smudge on her arm where she had rubbed against him. "I have the most awesome idea."

He looked down at her, and raised an eyebrow when she rubbed her hands together. For a moment, his eyes were frozen on the way they moved, as images of the night before danced through his head. Shaking it, he blinked and tried to focus on what she had said.

"What?" He asked.

Jordan took a step toward him just as the lift stopped and the door opened. "I said, I could bathe you, if you bathed me," she repeated with a toss of her head as she stepped out of the lift. "Last one in has to wash the other first."

Dagger stood staring at the back of Jordan as she took off. A low growl escaped him when he finally comprehended what she was saying. She was disappearing through the door to their cabin when the door to the lift started to close on him. Thrusting his hand out, he took off when it opened far enough for him to squeeze through.

He entered the room to a line of Jordan's clothing. It looked as if she had stripped on the move. Her ankle boots were tossed to the side. He stepped over the remains of the thin pajama 'shorts' she had made and her shirt. Turning, he paused when he heard the soft sound of her humming an unfamiliar song.

Pulling off his boots, he quickly stripped out of his clothing. He picked up his pants and Jordan's discarded clothes, and stuffed them in the clothing refresher before stepping into the doorway of the cleansing unit. For a moment, he just stood watching her as she lathered her long hair and tilted it back to rinse it.

"Are you coming in?" Her soft voice woke him from his trance and he nodded.

He pulled the door open and stepped inside with her. The shower was larger than normal for a Starship. Arindoss spared no expense when he upgraded the ship. It was either that, or the previous owner had just as an expensive taste as the former fight club owner. Right now, Dagger was just thankful for their forethought.

Dagger's eyes were glued to the moisture running down Jordan's upturned breasts. He bent forward, mesmerized by a stubborn droplet that clung to one taut nipple. Her low moan echoed in the narrow space when he ran his tongue over it.

"Let me," he murmured, taking the soap from her and squeezing a touch into the palm of his hand.

He didn't want anything between his skin and hers. Sliding his palms up under her breasts, he pressed a kiss to each nipple before running his hands over the rounded globes. The feel of his rough palms over her silky skin made him want more.

He followed the movement of his hands with his eyes, wanting to memorize every inch of her like this. The water on her skin made it glisten in the low lights of the cleansing unit. His fingers stroked her skin as he followed the tiny droplets.

Skimming his fingers over her stomach, he knelt in front of her. He gentle massaged the soap into her skin, watching as it dissolved and washed away. Raising his hand, he glanced up at her with a small, sexy smile.

"More," he ordered.

Jordan raised an eyebrow at him, but reached over and picked up the soap. Pouring another penny size drop in his hands, she wondered if she had made a mistake of challenging him when she almost dropped the bottle. She shifted her weight, leaning back against the back of the shower when he nudged her thighs in a command to open her legs for him.

"Dagger," she whispered throatily when he began massage the soft curls between her legs. "More. Use... Please..."

Another moan escaped her when he tugged on the curls. Her hips rotated until she was pressing them away from the wall and closer to him in invitation. She closed her eyes and sent a small prayer of thanks upward to the genius behind the alien soap that dissolved the moment the area was clean.

"Oh, yes," she whispered out loud when Dagger's lips replaced his fingers.

He murmured his approval when she raised her right leg and draped it over his shoulder while she held on to his shoulders. She leaned her head back and kept her eyes closed as she focused on the feelings rushing through her. Her hips rocked in rhythm with his tongue.

His eyes flickered upward when her left hand slid off his shoulder and to her breast. In his mind, he remembered what it was like to suck on them, pinch them until she arched upward for more. Just the thought of it made him want to come.

"Oh, Dagger," Jordan moaned when he slid his finger deep into her vaginal channel.

The silky smooth feel of her core wrapping around his finger sent pleasure bursting through him. He pulled almost all the way out, pulling a whimper from her and added another finger. She was tight and her body was greedy for him. Vivid memories of how it felt wrapping around his cock drew a silent curse from him and he renewed his attack on the small nub that he discovered caused her to shatter when he touched it.

He ran his tongue over it and was rewarded with a flow of her desire. Sliding his fingers through the light colored curls, he spread her labia, opening her to him. Reaching out, he touched the tip of his tongue to the small pebbled nub that seemed to swell in response. His hands pressed against her thighs when she jerked.

"Don't move," he growled against her.

Her low whimper was the only answer he received. He continued to lick the nub while stroking her, moving faster and faster in response to the pressure she was exerting on his shoulder and pressing against his back with her heel. He could feel the exact moment that she went over the edge into an explosive, soul shattering orgasm.

He twisted the two fingers he had pressed up inside her as she pulsed around him and drank deeply. The hand on her breast had dropped back down to his shoulder where she kneaded his flesh in time with her release. He reluctantly pulled back and rose on shaking legs.

Dagger threaded his fingers through her wet hair and sealed his lips against hers in a deep kiss. He knew that she could taste her essence on his lips. Deepening the kiss, his tongue danced with hers as he tried to show her how much her release had affected him.

Closing his eyes, he pulled back and rested his forehead against hers, drawing deep breathes to calm his thundering heart. He shuddered when he felt the tips of her fingers tracing the muscles of his stomach. Opening his eyes, he stared down at her in wonder.

"I love you," he whispered.

Jordan smiled tenderly up at him, her fingers moving in slow, sensual circles. "I love you, too. Now, it's my turn."

Dagger braced his arms against the side of the shower as Jordan poured a small portion of soap into her hand and rubbed them together before she began sliding them across his outstretched arms. He swallowed and bent his knees a little when she moved behind him and began rubbing his scalp before moving down to his shoulders.

"You're so much taller than me, I can't reach the top of your head without you bending down," she murmured, running her fingers along his shoulder once he had straightened.

"Does it bother you?" He asked, glancing over his shoulder. "My being taller than you?"

Jordan shook her head. "No," she replied, touching the faint scars crisscrossing his back. "No, I like it."

Dagger turned back around to face the wall. Jordan smiled when she saw his hand clench as she moved further down his body. Biting her bottom lip, she reached over and poured more soap into her palm before replacing it. Rubbing her hands together again, she took a step closer so that her breasts brush against his back while her hands slid down over his taut buttocks.

"I always did like a guy with a tight ass," she whispered as she ran her hands over the curve of his buttocks before circling around and cupping him in her hand. "Then, again, a nice crotch isn't so bad either."

Jordan could tell she was playing with fire. The tension building inside Dagger was radiating through the narrow shower unit. She knew he wouldn't last long, especially when she finally wrapped her hand around his cock.

She ran her hand back and forth along the slick, smooth surface. Her hand caught on the bulbous end and she circled it with her palm. The low, guttural groan that tore from his throat told her he had reached his limit. Twisting, his hands spanned her waist and lifted her up.

"Wrap your legs around my waist," he demanded, pressing her back against the other side of the shower unit.

His hands wrapped around her thighs as he drove upward, impaling her on his throbbing cock. Dagger leaned forward, breathing heavily into her ear as he rocked his hips. Each upward stroke drove him deeper into her. Jordan wrapped her arms around his neck and used her thigh muscles to help hold her still when his hands slid around her waist and pressed her more firmly against the shower wall.

Low, hiccuping sobs escaped her as he continued to drive in and out of her with increasing speed and force. Just when she thought her legs would give out, he threw his head back and cried out. Jordan bent forward, biting down on his shoulder as her own body reacted to the sudden swelling of his cock and the pulsing jet of his seed as he came.

"Yes!" He hissed, bowing his head against the curve of her neck. "Yes!"

Jordan laid her head against his shoulder in exhaustion. Her body felt limp, boneless, after such a joining. He kept one arm around her, holding her to him as he gently pulled out of her. A low whimper escaped her and she turned her face into his neck at the loss of their connection.

She was only vaguely aware of him turning off the shower. He stepped out of the shower with her still in his arms. Reaching for a towel, he set her on the vanity and tenderly dried her.

"Why don't you rest while I fix us something to eat?" He suggested, brushing her damp hair away from her face. "I will come get you when it is done."

Jordan blinked sleepily up at Dagger and nodded. A tired sigh escaped her when he picked her up and carried her into the other room. She was asleep before he even finished covering her up.

Dagger sat on the edge of the bed, watching Jordan for several long minutes before he finally stood up and pulled out a pair of clean trousers. Sliding them on, he didn't bother with his boots or a shirt. If he had his way, he wouldn't need them for the rest of the day.

Chapter 15

Dagger grunted and set down the tool he was using to work on the electrical system. At least the outside repairs were finally completed. It had taken him two days longer than he thought it would to fix it.

Part of the reason was because the damage was more extensive than he thought. The other part was because the narrow patch of dry ground they had taken refuge on was part of the Gartaians' feeding and mating ground. This made it impossible to do any work safely outside while the creatures were present.

"Here," Jordan said, handing him a bottle of water when he sat up. "At least we don't have to smell that creature anymore."

Dagger grimaced and nodded. "That's true," he replied, handing her back the empty bottle. "It took long enough for the others to clear the remains."

"Ew!" Jordan said, wiggling her nose.

Dagger laid back and picked up the splicer. The old bull had been no match for the younger one they discovered. The mammoth carcass had bloated in the heat. The other Gartaians took their time, stripping chucks from the decomposing body, but it hadn't been fast enough for him and Jordan.

"You should have stayed inside the ship," he grunted.

"And leave you unprotected out there while you worked? Not happening," she replied, taking a sip of her drink. "Besides, it didn't take them that long to clean it up."

Dagger chuckled. "No, it usually doesn't," he replied, liking the way humans shortened their words. "I need to finish this by today. The ship has sunk another foot. If we don't leave in the next day or so, I'm not sure we'll be able to without me digging out the landing gear."

"How much longer do you think it will take you?" Jordan asked.

"I need to check the connection on the outside panel. I didn't realize the circuit board was damaged, but I can see where it overheated and melted. Fortunately, I can repair it using components from another board. Still, I want to make sure it didn't melt through to the outside. If it did, it could cause an explosion during takeoff," he explained, sliding the damaged board out and laying it beside him.

"Why don't I go fix some dinner while you work on it?" Jordan asked, sliding her hand over his stomach. "You need to keep your strength up."

Dagger's hand whipped out and grabbed hers when she slid it lower. He watched her eyes darken and her face soften when he lifted his hips up at the same time as he pressed her hand down over his cock. This was something she had started the morning she smacked him on the ass. Foreplay, she called it. Whatever the hell it was, he enjoyed it.

"Kiss me," he ordered, pulling her hand up and toward him so that she twisted off balance and half fell across him. "Kiss me, Jordan."

He released her hand and slid his palm down and over her hip. Meeting her half way, the playful kiss turned to heated desire. He swore the more they came together, the more he wanted.

"I definitely think you need to be fed," she whispered, lying almost completely on top of him.

"Warning, vessel alert," the computer suddenly announced.

"Ouch!" Jordan cursed when she jerked her head up in surprise and it hit the underside of the console. "What the...."

Dagger rolled Jordan off of him and twisted. He jumped to his feet before reaching down and helping her up. A low curse exploded from his lips at the thought of how defenseless they were. Pulling her behind him, he strode toward the door.

"How far out?" He demanded as he reached for the laser rifle propped up next to the door of the engine room. "Give me the estimated time of arrival."

"Fifteen meters, the vessel is currently landing," the computer replied.

"That's impossible," Dagger muttered under his breath as they stepped into the lift. "Starship classification and weapon systems analysis."

"Unknown," the computer replied.

"Damn it," Dagger growled, glancing at Jordan's wide worried eyes.

"What is it?" She asked, biting her lip. "I thought the computer was supposed to give us more notice."

"It should have," he stated, slipping through the door and pulling her behind him as he headed for the bridge. "Computer..."

Dagger's voice faded as he looked out of the front view screen. He had been about to demand a self-test on the system to make sure there wasn't a malfunction in the circuitry, but that order died on his lips when he looked out the front of the Starship.

There was no fault in the system. The computer was right, there was a vessel landing. It was also correct about one other fact. He didn't know what the hell it was either.

Before the *Lexamus IV* was the strangest looking Starship he had ever seen. The vessel shifted, changing forms as it rotated in place before landing on the soft surface. He watched in disbelief as large rows of dark red crystal formed and connected to make a wide flat base, so the vessel didn't sink down. The structure instead distributed the weight across the surface. Shimmering red crystals reflected the bright light of the mid-afternoon sun.

If Dagger thought the ship was bizarre, it was nothing compared to what came out of it when a door and steps appeared from nowhere out of the side of it. He was vaguely aware of Jordan leaning forward with a frown as she studied what was happening as well. They both watched as two men and what appeared to be a robot and a half, descended the steps. The men appeared to be having a heated conversation from the way they were talking and the waving of their hands. What was stranger was they didn't appear to be carrying any weapons.

"Are those…." Jordan stared for a moment more. "Those look like humans!"

"Yes, they do," Dagger growled under his breath and turned.

Jordan straightened and stared at him as he picked up a weapons belt and slid it on before he gripped the laser rifle in his hand again. He could hear her following him as he strode off the bridge. A dark scowled of concern swept across his face when she stepped into the lift behind him.

"What are you going to do?" She asked breathlessly.

"Go introduce myself and find out where in the hell they came from," Dagger muttered.

* * *

"I told you, we should have taken a left at that last star!" Luc argued. "I do not know why Jarmen will not listen to me!"

"It is because you have drunk too much wine," Jon Paul retorted. "The last star on the left! That is a children's tale, Luc. We are trying to get back to Earth, not find the Pirate Captain Hook!"

"Ah, well, it was better than finding out we went too far like we did at that last place," Luc replied, turning to look at the two robots following slowly behind them. "Isn't that right, Numbnuts? They almost tore you apart, eh, my friend?"

"Yes, Dumbass, the local inhabitants were not familiar with the workings of a Class A Service Bot," Numbnuts stated, pulling one leg out of the muck when he began to sink only to find that his other leg was now sinking.

"I think we should have asked for an owner's manual of the ship before we stole it, if you ask me," the small robot muttered, kicking up a patch of mud under the wheels attached to his feet. "This mud is not doing a thing for my wheels."

"I think I liked you better before he re-programmed you, IQ. You were more fun," Luc muttered. "Do you think that thing even has an owner's manual, Jon Paul?"

Jon Paul stopped and shrugged. "How should I know? I don't know anything about Starships. You know that," he responded, before tilting his head. "Something tells me Jarmen is hoping that we do not come back?"

"Why do you say that?" Luc asked, turning as the figure of a male suddenly appeared from the other Spaceship.

Jon Paul shifted uneasily from one foot to the other when he saw the weapon aimed at them, not to mention the other weapons around the male's waist. If that wasn't enough to make him want to piss in his pants, the air of menace combined with the ragged scar across the man's cheek that made him look even more intimidating, and the look of death in his eyes, confirmed it.

"We should not have upset, Jarmen," Jon Paul whispered, slowly raising his arms.

Luc glanced at his friend and lover and raised his hands as well. "But, it was IQ who suggested asking for directions, not me this time," Luc choked out, watching with wide eyes as the man stopped less than ten feet in front of them.

"Bonjour, monsieur. I am Jon Paul and this is Luc," Jon Paul stuttered. "Would you happen to know what year it is back on Earth?"

"Dagger, they *are* human!" A soft voice exclaimed behind the man.

* * *

Dagger watched the two men as they raised their hands into the air. Both wore a lopsided grin and were staring back at him with wide, brown eyes filled with curiosity more than fear. He deduced that part of the reason for their lack of fear was Jordan's smiling face.

"Jordan," he hissed when she took a step forward and held out her hand, giggling when one of the men raised it to his lips and kissed the back of it.

She glanced over her shoulder and frown. "They're human, Dagger," she replied with a touch of admonishment.

"I know they are human," he retorted in a low voice, lowering his weapon when she crossed in front of it. "What I want to know is how they got here?"

"I can explain that, monsieur," Jon Paul replied with an easy grin. "Our host, a most disagreeable, ill-tempered man named Jarmen D'ju wished for us to ask for directions."

"Yes," Luc agreed with an eager nod. "We are lost again. We are not sure what time period we have arrived in."

"Luc!" Jon Paul scolded, turning on Luc and rambling a long sentence in a different language before he turned back and smiled apologetically at Dagger. "I apologize. We were only instructed to find out the date and confirm our location. Our friend is still learning how to drive the Crystal ship."

Dagger opened his mouth to reply, but closed it when another figure appeared in the doorway of the red Crystal ship. His eyes narrowed on the male. He was several inches shorter than Dagger, yet there was an air of strength and power in his stance. The male returned his stare without blinking.

"Monsieur, may I present, Jarmen D'ju," Jon Paul replied with a sigh. "He is the captain."

"He doesn't have a sense of humor," Luc whispered, leaning closer to Jordan and rolling his eyes. "I think he has a stick up his ass, eh."

"I do not have a stick up my ass, Luc," the male stated as he walked closer. "I have already told you that before."

Dagger watched as Luc turned away from Jarmen and rolled his eyes again. Jordan had pressed her lips together when Luc mouthed that he 'did too have a stick up his ass. A very large one'. Dagger raised an eyebrow at the teasing comment. He had to give Luc credit. The human was either extremely brave or he had a death wish.

"Who are you and what are you doing here?" Dagger demanded, tightening his grip on the rifle in his hand.

Dagger watched as Jarmen D'ju's eyes flickered over the movement before he dismissed it. Instead, the man's eyes began to glow an unusual red. Unease built in Dagger as the man remained silent for several long seconds.

"You have a burnt electrical circuit in engine two. The power crystals for the left thrusters are also depleted," Jarmen replied instead. "There are minor component error messages that need to be resolved before the ship is safe for flight. I will help you with the repairs in exchange for information."

"Who the hell are you and where did you come from?" Dagger demanded, pulling Jordan behind him and stepping back.

"He is harmless, monsieur," Jon Paul said hastily when he saw the alarm on Dagger's face. "He can…"

"He is half robot," Luc interjected with a shrug. "He is on a quest."

Dagger studied the faces of the men for several long seconds before they narrowed on Jarmen's face. The man's eyes were shuttered and his face devoid of expression. The only indication that he might be annoyed was the small tick in his jaw.

"What kind of quest?" Dagger asked suspiciously.

"Love," Luc and Jon Paul answered at the same time.

"Not love," Jarmen retorted finally before he turned to look at Dagger. "There was an error in my calculations. We… arrived in orbit around the planet. The Crystal ship's scans picked up your ship.

Identification of it indicated that your ship might contain the star charts I need."

"What are you looking for?" Jordan asked softly, placing her hand on Dagger's arm so that he would lower the weapon he had started to lift.

For a moment, Dagger caught the fleeting anguish in the other man's eyes. Man or robot, this man was looking for someone. If what the other two men said was true, it was someone that meant a great deal to him.

"Jane," Jarmen replied, looking a Jordan. "Her name is Jane and she is from a planet called Earth."

* * *

Jordan watched in fascination as the two Frenchmen talked while they prepared a meal aboard the *Lexamus IV* an hour later. It had taken some fancy talking and finally the realization that the three men and their robots were not a threat when the two men began arguing again, this time in French with each other.

Jordan had fallen in love with them when the large robot called Numbnuts walked up behind both men and lifted them by the back of their shirts. The little robot, called IQ, explained that their 'weird friend' Jarmen had programed Numbnuts to keep the two men from getting hurt.

"So, are you attached, in a relationship, seeing anyone?" IQ asked, walking his fingers up Jordan's arm.

A chuckle escaped Luc when he heard the little robot. He turned twinkling eyes to Jordan, who was giggling. The grin on his face widened when he saw a set of irritated red eyes, almost the color of their ship, turn to glare at him. With another laugh, he turned with a glass of wine for each of them.

"I told Jon Paul that I liked his programming better than Jarmen's," Luc replied with a wink as he set a glass down in front of Jordan with a bow. "Only the best wine for my beautiful lady."

Jordan picked up the wine and looked at it. She had never drunk any alcoholic beverages before. When the world went crazy, that seemed to be the most prized commodity for a lot of people. Shrugging at Dagger's raised eyebrow, she lifted the drink and took a sip. A shudder of distaste made her face scrunch up and she wiggled her nose at it.

Dagger's low chuckle made her blush. She turned when the little robot climbed up on the table and lay down in front of her with one gangly, metal three-fingered hand under his chin. She grinned and leaned forward to brush a kiss across its brow.

"IQ, off the table," Jarmen ordered with a low growl. "Jon Paul, you should not change his programming."

"But, I think he is adorable," Jordan said, sitting back in her seat when she suddenly found the small robot in her lap. "Oh!"

"You shouldn't encourage him," Jarmen said, tilting his head. "He…"

"Jane liked him the way Jon Paul programmed him, as well," Luc interrupted when he saw Jarmen's eyes beginning to glow. "He made her laugh."

Jordan saw the flash of pain across the strange man's face before it returned to the blank mask. She glanced at Dagger and knew he had seen the reaction as well. Whoever Jane was, she really meant a lot to the man.

"Here, a feast fit for a beautiful princess," Jon Paul said, walking over to the table and setting down a tray. "The food on this ship is much better than what we have."

"So is the wine, eh?" Luc moaned as he sniffed his glass before sipping it.

Jordan bit her lip, staring at the two men, as IQ lifted her fork to her mouth. She automatically opened her mouth to accept the bite of food before taking the fork from the little robot when Jarmen growled at it again to get down. The little bot huffed and grumbled, but he climbed off her lap and rolled away.

"Where are you two from?" Jordan asked Luc and Jon Paul.

"Canada, then the stars," they both said at the same time. Luc chuckled and waved to Jon Paul to continue as he picked up his wine glass. "You are a much better storyteller than I, Jon Paul."

"It was a clear and beautiful starlit sky in September," Jon Paul began.

"No, no, it was cloudy and raining," Luc interrupted with a frown. "And it was in the Spring."

Jon Paul glared across the table at Luc and pointed his knife at him. "You said I could tell the story, so I will tell the story the way I want to," Jon Paul stated with a glare. "I want it to be a beautiful, starlit night and so it shall be a beautiful, starlit night this time."

Luc took another sip of wine and leaned toward Jordan with a wink. "It was early spring and raining," he whispered. "Go on, I will listen to your starlit story."

* * *

Dagger glanced at the two Frenchmen, listening with half an ear as they tried to charm Jordan. He would have felt jealous if he had not discovered that the two men were, in fact, in love with each other. Turning his attention back to the man across from him, he contemplated how he should handle the situation. He knew that the male wasn't being completely honest with him, yet he didn't sense any threat from him or his 'crew' of misfits. He believed Jarmen when he said he was looking for a woman named Jane

"Are they always like that?" He asked, taking a bite of the food that the men had prepared. His eyes widened at the burst of flavors and he glanced at the two animated figures that were competing for Jordan's attention now. "This is good."

"Yes, and that is the only reason that I haven't killed them… yet," Jarmen stated calmly.

Something told Dagger that the male meant it. He turned when Jordan's laughter rang out. His eyes widening when he saw that she was sipping more of the wine. His brow creased when he saw Luc innocently top it off when she set it back down on the table.

"Where did you get your ship?" Dagger asked bluntly, turning back to Jarmen.

Jarmen returned Dagger's intense stare. "I stole it," he replied. "I needed it, so I took it."

"Why did you need it? Where did you steal it from and are the ones you stole it from going to come looking for it here?" Dagger demanded, clutching his fist around the knife in his hand. "I won't allow anyone to put Jordan in any more danger than she already is."

Jarmen's hand moved in a blur of speed. The knife in Dagger's hand disappeared and reappeared in Jarmen's. Dagger watched as the male twirled the knife between his fingers before turning it and holding it back out to him. It was a clear message that if he had wanted to harm them, he would have done so already. Dagger carefully took the utensil and set it down next to his plate.

"I am no threat to you or the female," Jarmen replied, confirming what Dagger had been thinking. "The only ones in danger are the Frenchmen and their robots. No one will search for the Ship. I cannot tell you any more about where the ship came from, what it is, or when I am going. If I did not need their assistance, I would leave those two with you. Unfortunately, I will need their assistance once I arrive at my destination."

"You know that the Earth is under the Trivator and Alliance protection," Dagger informed him. "You will need to get permission granted to land."

"Not when I am going," Jarmen replied dismissively. "I have completed a more thorough scan of your ship. I will help you complete the repairs before I leave in return for your assistance in keeping those two away from me for a short period of time."

"Why don't you just leave without them?" Dagger asked, turning to watch Jordan as she snorted into her hand at something Luc said.

"Sorry!" She whispered before bursting into giggles again. "Sorry!"

Amusement tugged at his lips. His little mate was tipsy. "On second thought, don't," he murmured when the two men began to sing in an off-key melody.

Jarmen turned to gaze at the two men who were working their way through the third bottle of wine. It was true, if he hadn't needed their help, he would have left them behind back on Kassis. Neither one had given him much choice. They had both told him either he took them, and the robots, with him on his quest or they would inform the Kassisan leader, Torak Ja Kel Coradon that he planned on stealing the Crystal ship that belonged to the people of Elpidios.

The real reason is I know that Jane will accept them before she would ever accept me, he thought.

No, as much as he hated to admit that he actually needed the help of the two men, he needed to find Jane before he lost her forever.

Chapter 16

Dagger released a silent chuckle when Jordan's soft snores echoed in the corridor as he picked her up. She had curled up on the narrow padded seat about a half hour before and fallen asleep. He paused when Jarmen walked out into the corridor behind him.

"I will take you up on your offer to leave those two here for the night, as well as the robots," Jarmen stated in a calm voice. "I would spend more time trying to keep them alive if I try to take them back to the Crystal ship, and I might forget why I should."

The chuckle he had been fighting to hold back escaped when Jordan's arm rose and she tried to roll in his arms. The two Frenchmen were asleep on the floor of the dining area while the two robots had plugged themselves into the *Lexamus* power grid. There was still a lot he didn't understand about Jarmen D'Ju, but he felt confident that neither he nor the two humans were a threat.

"The Gartaians will be feeding at this time of night," Dagger warned him. "It would be safer for you to remain here."

Jarmen shook his head, glancing back at the dining area where a duet of rumbling snores echoed. "I will not have difficulty returning to the Crystal ship," he assured Dagger. "It will be pleasant to have quiet so that I may work on my calculations."

"Good luck," Dagger said, grimacing when Jordan shifted again and burrowed into his chest. "I must put my tipsy mate to bed."

Dagger watched as Jarmen walked down the corridor and stepped into the lift. There were several things he wanted to do before he called it a night. First though, was the care of his mate.

Stepping through the open door to their room, he ordered the door to lock behind him. It didn't take long for him to remove her clothing and settle her under the covers. He sat on the edge of the bed and ran his hand down the silky strands of her hair.

"I love you, Jordan Sampson," he whispered.

Tonight, he had seen her in a different light. She had been happy, animated in a way he had never seen before. Her eyes had continuously sought him out, and he hadn't missed the shy smile of happiness or the teasing looks the two Frenchmen kept casting his way.

"I would have you laugh like you did tonight for the rest of your life," he whispered before releasing a sigh and standing.

Walking over to the door, he ordered it to open. He jumped in surprise when the little robot called IQ wobbled on its wheels before blinking up at him as if it was sleepy. He knew that was impossible.

His eyebrow rose when it rolled pass him to the bed where Jordan lay sleeping. Within seconds, it had climbed up on the bed and curled into a ball next to her. Shaking his head, Dagger wondered what the hell strange world he had woken up into.

* * *

The next morning, he watched as Jordan came down the rear platform to where he and Jarmen were finishing up the final repairs. She was still walking very carefully and had found a pair of dark goggles in one of the panels in the bedroom.

"Bonjour, Madam Jordan," Luc called out in a cheerful voice.

Jordan raised one hand in greeting and the other to her head. Dagger bent his head to hide the smile of amusement. He fitted the panel back in place while Jarmen used the drill to tighten it down.

"Remind me to never drink alcohol again," Jordan whispered when she reached where they were working. "I can't believe one glass could make me feel this way."

Dagger chuckled. "It was more like one bottle," he murmured, pressing a tender kiss to her temple. "Luc kept refilling your glass."

Jordan's eyes widened behind the dark glass and she glanced at where the two Frenchmen and Numbnuts were digging the soil out from around the last landing foot of the *Lexamus IV*. A sigh escaped her and she moaned when she tried to shake her head. Unwilling for her to continue the morning in pain, he called out for IQ to come to him.

"Don't…," Jordan hissed, pressing her trembling fingers to her forehead. "Please, don't yell."

"IQ, take Jordan to the medical unit and have her lay down in it," Dagger ordered in a softer voice.

"I'll take care of my girl," IQ replied in an exaggerated whispered. "Come on, my beloved. Let IQ take all your pain away."

Jordan gave Dagger a wan smile before turning and following the little robot back up the platform. He had ordered the two Frenchman this morning to take the remaining liquor back to their Starship. He didn't think the two men could move so fast. They had been so grateful, they hadn't complained when Jarmen ordered them to dig out around the landing feet.

"Thank you for your help," Dagger said, turning back to Jarmen.

Jarmen shrugged. "You needed assistance, and it keeps those two and the robots out of trouble," he replied before his eyes began to glow and his mouth tightened. "Your scanner has indicated that four Starships are approaching the planet."

Dagger swore under his breath. "How long before they are in range?" He asked, picking up the tools and moving up the platform.

"Within the hour," Jarmen commented. "These are the ones that you told me about last night?"

"Possibly," Dagger replied. "I need to see what type of ships they are. I haven't contacted any of my people for fear that the signal would be intercepted. I couldn't risk it with the ship being damaged."

Jarmen turned to Luc and Jon Paul. "Return to the Crystal Ship and prepare for departure," he ordered. He turned as IQ came rolling down the platform at high speed. "The female?"

"Healed," IQ replied before he rolled himself into a tight ball and sped toward the red ship.

"Dagger, the computer said…," Jordan called out in an urgent voice from the top of the platform.

"Get strapped in," Dagger said, grabbing the last of the tools. "What type?"

Jarmen shook his head. "Not military," he replied, his eyes glowed with a deep, dark red. "Interception of transmission between them is difficult due to non-compatible programming. Recalculating…." Jarmen stood frozen for a moment before he blinked. "They are using a jamming device, but I was able to pick out one name that you mentioned last night."

Dagger could feel his muscles tighten in anticipation. His jaw clenched as he waited for Jarmen to confirm what he already felt in his gut. They had been found.

"Kelman," Jarmen replied.

* * *

"Buckle in," Dagger demanded as he slid into the pilot seat. "*Red One*, this is the *Lexamus*, you are clear for departure."

"*Red One*, clear," Jarmen's voice responded.

Jordan watched as the Crystal Ship rose off the ground. She knew her mouth was hanging open when the platform of red crystals rose up and blended into the Starship. Closing her mouth, she watched as Dagger prepared their Starship for departure.

"Are you strapped in?" He asked, briefly glancing at her before he returned his attention to the front panel.

"Yes," she whispered before clearing her throat. "Yes. What about the power? I know that the left thrusters were depleted."

"I don't know what Jarmen did, but he was able to recharge them while I worked on the electricals," Dagger replied.

"Dagger, fighters have been dispersed and are coming in at a high rate of speed," Jarmen reported. "I will engage them while you lift off. Be prepared for a battle."

"Kill them," Dagger ordered.

"Of course," Jarmen replied before the transmission ended.

Jordan bit her thumb as they began to rise off the ground. A shadow caught her attention out of her right peripheral vision and she turned as the young bull Gartaian burst out of the wooded swamp. She gasped when it rose up and roared.

"Dagger," she cried out, reaching out to him.

Dagger nodded grimly to let her know that he had seen the creature as well. Pressing down on the control, he pulled down on the level. There was a slight resistance as the ship pulled out of the thin layer of muck that had settled back around the landing gear. All at once, he felt the ship break free and began to rise.

The creature below had fallen forward again and was crossing the river at a rapid pace. Jordan scooted back in her seat as the image of the creature became larger the closer he approached. A low whimper of relief escaped her when the *Lexamus* suddenly shot forward and down the narrow meadow.

"That was close," she murmured before she covered her mouth to keep from crying out when the trees in front of them exploded.

"Hang on," Dagger growled, tilting the *Lexamus* away from the blasts that were exploding around them. "*Red One....*"

"I'm on him," Jarmen replied.

Jordan leaned forward and watched as a flash of red curved around and came toward them, firing at the ship behind them. The *Lexamus* passed under it and continued to rise. Glancing sideways, she saw Dagger's grim expression and knew that there were more.

"What can I do?" Jordan asked in a husky voice.

Dagger briefly glanced at her before returning his attention to the view in front of him. "You said you were a gamer," he replied. "How good are you at shooting things?"

Jordan's lips curved and her eyes gleamed with determination. "The best," she answered confidently.

Dagger's hand flashed to a control on the screen in front of him. Jordan's eyes widened when another screen appeared in front of her. She recognized the different weapons and the view of those chasing them. It wasn't unlike some of the games she had played before, well, the graphics were a lot better, but she knew what to do.

"I'm on it," she said, focusing on the screen.

Her fingers swept through the weapons. Choosing the rear pulse cannon, she locked and loaded it. It would work better on the smaller, more mobile fighters that had been sent after them. Her eyes followed the target as it swept back and forth. The moment it came into the cross arrows, she fired.

The rearview scan showed the fighter exploding. She didn't bother celebrating, but instead focused on the next fighter that appeared. They were like a swarm of bees. She concentrated on keeping them at bay.

"Oh, no you don't, you asshole," Jordan bit out under her breath when she saw seven more appear on her radar. "You are so going down."

* * *

Dagger didn't take his eyes off the screen. While the *Lexamus* was larger than the fighters and not quite as mobile, it was more powerful. Sweeping up over the ledge of rock where the cave was that he originally hoped to use was located; he banked before dropping down into a wide canyon. The maneuver forced the fighters behind them into a single formation.

In the corner of his eye, he saw another fighter break apart. Jordan was damn good as a weapons officer. She wasn't lying when she said she was the best. He knew few warriors that could do as well.

"We need to get out of here," he said. "*Red One,* I'm reading six fighters."

"Three," Jarmen replied as multiple explosions took out the last three in the line following them. "I am still learning the controls of the Crystal ship."

"I'm taking us up and out," Dagger said, not responding to Jarmen's comment. "There will be the four ships waiting for us to break through. Expect more fighters."

"Affirmative," Jarmen responded.

Dagger glanced at the screen as another fighter disintegrated. Jordan had struck again. A flash showed the shields were at ninety-eight percent and holding.

"Uh, Dagger," Jordan said, glancing up as the huge red wall of rock in front of them came closer and closer. "There's a wall."

"I know," he said.

Dagger's eyes flickered to the two fighters behind them before glancing back up. The pilots of the fighters were weaving back and forth, staying just far enough that pulse cannons wouldn't work on them. Gritting his teeth, he counted down until he was close enough to pull up and glide over the plateau at the top.

At the top, the *Lexamus* swept past the Jarmen's Crystal ship. The fighters, not expecting the other ship to be waiting, were defenseless when it opened fire on them. Both fighters exploded and fell back into the canyon in a raging ball of fire.

"What now?" Jordan asked, glancing at the weapons and trying to decide which would be the best.

"Now, we see just how fast this ship can go," Dagger replied grimly. "Computer, maximum shields."

"Shields at maximum," the computer responded.

The *Lexamus* surged forward, breaking through the thin atmosphere of the planet. Four Starships were positioned off the small planet waiting for them. Dagger increased the speed of *Lexamus* as they opened fire. They had strategically positioned themselves in an effort to block Dagger from escaping.

Dagger's eyes widened when the red Crystal ship exploded past the *Lexamus*. A loud curse tore from his lips when he saw it shimmer for a moment. He was vaguely aware of Jordan's low cry of dismay as Jarmen aimed his ship at the largest Starship.

Fighters had begun to pour out of the massive ship, but didn't get far as the Crystal ship passed directly through the body of the huge modified Warship. Within seconds, the Crystal ship appeared on the other side, undamaged. It left behind a huge gaping hole in the mercenary's largest ship.

It took a few seconds for it to register what had happened, once it did, Dagger knew that the ship would implode. The force would be devastating to anything close to it. Swiping his hand over the control, he pushed the *Lexamus* engines to the max in an effort to get as far away as possible as the attack ship imploded sending rippling shocks waves and millions of pieces of debris outward.

"How did he do that?" Jordan whispered, her hand going to her throat.

"I don't know," Dagger replied, punching in the coordinates for a jump to light speed. *"Red One,* this is *Lexamus IV,* status report."

The sound of cursing, in French, was very loud in the background. From the sound of it, everyone aboard the Crystal ship was alive and well. Well, at least for a short period, if Jarmen's growl for the men to shut up was anything to go by.

"The largest attack ship has been destroyed along with the fighters. Two of the other ships were severely damaged in the explosion from the readings I have so far. I will destroy the last ship before I depart," Jarmen responded.

"I don't know how you did that and survived, but I sure as hell wish I had a ship like that," Dagger muttered. "Thank you again for your help, Jarmen."

"I need a drink," Luc groaned in the background. "I am definitely a lover and not a fighter."

Jordan giggled as the transmission ended. She looked at Dagger with bright, shining eyes and grinned. Hope and relief battled in them, as well, as she stared at him.

"Can we go home?" She asked in a husky voice.

Dagger nodded. "Yes, my brave warrior," he replied, turning back to the controls. "Yes, we will return to Rathon and our home; but, there is someplace I need to take you to first."

Chapter 17

"Report," Kelman demanded, staring out at the remains of his attack ships.

"There were no survivors," the man standing behind him reported. "Whatever did this made sure of that. We do have a track on the energy signature that jumped to light speed. Do you want us to follow it?"

"Yes," Kelman replied.

He ignored the man as he turned and departed the small room that Kelman used off the bridge of the warship he had commandeered from a Tearnat shortly after the war ended between them and the Kassisans. His eyes swept over the area of space littered with a good size chunk of his wealth. He had ordered the other warships to move ahead after they had searched the last planet.

Kelman's hand rose to rub the smooth stone at his neck. He would have been on his flagship if not for the delay at the mining colony. It was one of his and he had discovered while he was there that the warden of the operations was stealing from him. He made a practice of personally handling anyone that stole from him. That decision had saved his life.

"You will go home," Kelman whispered to himself. A slow, menacing smile curved his lips. "It will be challenging, but not impossible."

Turning, he stepped up to the console on the center of the desk. Tapping out a command, he waited for a response. It took only a minute before it came through.

'*Yes,*' was all the message said.

Satisfied, he turned back to the window as the warship picked up speed, leaving the debris behind. The Trivator named Dagger owed him. Kelman had to call in a debt, something he didn't like having to do. People tended to think they didn't owe him anything else once he did that. What they didn't know was that he owned them for the rest of their lives.

"Yes, you owe me," Kelman whispered. "Not just in lost revenue and for the destruction of my property, but for thinking you could escape me. You have a weakness, my fighter, a weakness that will be your downfall."

The female would be a prize that he would cherish. She would keep the large Trivator under his control. He wouldn't kill her, but that didn't mean that she was immune to what would happen if the Trivator tried to rebel. In his mind, he could still see the haunted look and the anger burning in the Trivator's eyes when he tenderly picked the wounded female up off the ground back on Bruttus.

"Yes, you have a weakness, and I plan to use it against you," Kelman murmured thoughtfully.

* * *

Jordan bit her lip and looked at Dagger's stony face. They had made the jump into light speed over an hour ago and were heading toward the outer regions of the star system where Dagger said a Jump Gate was located. She watched as he waited for his brother to answer the signal he had sent out. Now that the *Lexamus* was back in tiptop condition, Dagger told her that he felt more confident about using the communications system to contact his brother.

"Where are you?" Trig demanded. "Is Jordan alright?"

Dagger's face darkened at the reminder that Trig had been the one responsible for bringing Jordan to Bruttus. His hand curled into a fist when he remembered everything that had happened and how close he had come to losing her. The fact that she had been the one to free him wasn't forgotten, but neither was the fact that she had been in the position to do so.

"I'm going to kill you," Dagger quietly told his brother. "You should never have taken her with you."

"Dagger," Jordan reproached in a soft voice.

"You are safe," Trig's relieved voice sounded over the console. "Where are you?"

"Hi, Trig," Jordan responded. "Yes, I'm safe. I'm with Dagger and I have no clue where we are."

"What happened?" Trig asked.

Dagger's fist that had started to relax clenched again. "I'll tell you what happened, Jordan almost died," he bit out in a harsh voice. "What were you thinking, taking her to Bruttus. You know better than anyone what could have happened to her."

Silence greeted his statement. "I'm sorry, brother," Trig finally replied. "I should have protected her better."

"I didn't give you much of a choice," Jordan pointed out, turning in her seat to look at Dagger. "I didn't, Dagger. You should know that by now. I told

Trig that I would find another way to get to you, and I would have. Trig did everything he could to protect me, including calling for assistance. Without the help of Kali and the other Trivators, I would never have been able to get you out. Did… Is Kali, Sword, and the others… Did they make it out safely?"

"Yes," Trig replied with a gruff laugh. "Razor came close to killing Sword, Race, and Cannon, but they made it out in one piece. What about Kelman? We searched for him after Razor and the others killed the Drethulan. The fight ring is shut down and Razor ordered a cleansing of the Spaceport. Additional troops are being sent in to clean up the area. It has been neglected for too long. I guess kidnapping a High Chancellor of the Alliance woke the others up to what could happen to them, not to mention the alliance between our worlds, if they didn't agree. Razor was ready to blow the entire Spaceport up."

"What stopped him?" Dagger asked, rubbing absently at his wrist as he remembered what it felt like to be chained there.

"Kali," Trig retorted with a sigh. "She pointed out that there were a lot of merchants that lived there and were trying to make a legal living. Razor left Sword to oversee the cleanup."

"Kelman may still be alive. I don't know if he was on any of the attack ships that were destroyed," Dagger replied. "My gut is telling me that he is still alive. Tell Razor I want a bounty on Kelman's head."

"Already done," Trig replied. "The problem is, everyone capable of carrying it out either works for Kelman or is too afraid to try."

Dagger's face twisted in disgust. "Tell Hunter that I will return with Jordan to Rathon shortly. I... I need time," he said, casting a glance at Jordan. "I need time with my *Amate*."

The silence this time was different, lighter. "I'm happy for you, brother," Trig replied. "I will inform Hunter. Is there anything you need? If Kelman is out there, do you think it safe to stay away? I can provide coverage if you need time, from a safe distance."

"No," Dagger responded in a quiet voice. "We will be safe where I am going. He would not be so reckless or stupid to go where we are heading."

"Safe travels, brother," Trig finally replied. "Keep in contact, though."

"I will," Dagger said. "Out."

Dagger programmed the auto-pilot and rose from his seat. Reaching out his hand, he waited. Jordan's soft palm slid across his and he pulled her up and into his arms. Only then, did he feel the tension dissolve from his body. A rush of emotion swamped him when he thought of the danger she had been in once again.

"I want you," he muttered. "I just... want you."

Jordan understood what he was saying without really saying it. Her heart swelled when he looked down at her. The mixture of emotion told her that he was fighting the demons inside him once again. The demon that made him feel out of control and vulnerable. His fear that he might still wake up and find that this had all been a dream.

Pulling out of his arms, she clasped his hand in hers and pulled him toward the doorway. They walked in silence, both lost in their thoughts.

* * *

Rathon: Two years ago.

Jordan knew she was blushing, but she couldn't help it nor did she care. A transport was lowering itself in the front courtyard of Jesse and Hunter's house and she immediately recognized one of the figures in it. Dagger.

They had only been on Rathon a few weeks, but he came by every day. Today, he was going to show her around. She watched as Taylor ran out to the transport. As usual, her little sister was doing everything she could to drive Saber crazy.

"I think that is my new mission in life," Taylor had commented earlier this morning when she came out wearing a pair of tight short-shorts and a halter top. "The big lug needs someone to stir the ice in his veins and see that life is full of wonderful things... like me."

Taylor had recently turned sixteen and was beginning to really blossom. Personally, Jordan didn't think it was ice running through Saber's veins, but bubbling lava at Taylor's constant teasing. Taylor's loud squeal made Jordan chuckle under her breath and push away from the window. Saber had noticed Taylor's outfit and had scooped her little sister up into his arms. They were currently making a beeline for the front door.

"You will change into something appropriate," Saber snarled as he carried Taylor through the door.

"I am wearing something appropriate," Taylor snapped back, glaring up at Saber's stony face. "It's called shorts and a halter top. The girls wore them back home all the time."

"I don't remember seeing any of the women wearing them," Dagger said with a frown. "I'm sure I would have remembered if they did."

"Maybe only the children did," Saber snapped, lowering Taylor to her feet inside the door. "Not a grown female. You will change before any other males see you like this."

Jordan knew there was about to be a battle of wills from the way Taylor tossed her head back and folded her arms across her chest. She reminded Jordan of their grandmother when she was arguing with their dad. Her dad never won when her grandma was in a mood.

"Well, since you think I'm only a 'child', then I guess it's okay to wear it," Taylor pointed out cheekily. "Hi, Dagger."

"Greetings, Taylor," Dagger said with a grin. "Is…"

Jordan flushed again when Dagger's voice faded when he saw her. She smiled shyly at him and stepped farther into the foyer. Casting a gaze at Taylor, she knew her younger sister was silently begging her to support her.

"It's true, Saber," Jordan remarked in a quiet voice. "Women of all ages wear shorts and tops like that. I had several of each before…."

Jordan bit her lip and lowered her head. It was still difficult for her to talk about what happened after the Trivators landed on Earth. She started when she felt a gentle hand slid over her cheek. Blinking, she realized that Saber and Taylor were still arguing, but that they had walked into the other room.

"I am afraid I would have to agree with Saber," Dagger said in a low voice.

Jordan blinked in confusion. "About… About what?" She asked in a slightly breathless voice that made her cringe. "What would you agree with Saber about?" She repeated in a stronger voice.

"I would not want any other males to see you dressed in such clothing," he chuckled. "I would not mind, though, seeing you in it for myself."

"Oh," Jordan whispered, blushing like crazy.

Note to self, she thought as she stared up at him. *I need to get Hunter's mom to help me make several sets of shorts and halter tops.*

"Are you ready?" Dagger asked, sliding his hand around to the small of her back.

"Ready for what?" A dark voice asked from behind them.

Jordan turned slightly into Dagger when she heard Hunter's voice. Jesse was walking up to stand beside him. She looked at her older sister with pleading eyes. Just like Taylor needed her support, she needed Jesse's right now.

"I promised to show Jordan around," Dagger replied.

Jordan returned her new brother-in-law's searching gaze. She had discovered that on Rathon the rules were slightly different than on Earth. Each female was protected by their family. In their case, since they did not have any males to protect them, Hunter assumed the role when he claimed Jesse. That role included denying any warrior that might approach him and who showed an interest in her or Taylor.

"I think that is a wonderful idea," Jesse said with a grin. "She hasn't been out very much."

Hunter turned and frowned down at Jesse. "Jesse," he started to argue before he released a sigh of resignation. He glanced over at Dagger with a look of warning in his eyes. "I hold you responsible if anything should happen to her. She is still too young, Dagger. It is my right, as well as my responsibility, to make sure she is protected."

Dagger bowed his head in acknowledgement of the warning in Hunter's voice. "I will protect her with my life, Hunter, you need not worry," he promised. "Jesse."

"Have fun," Jesse called, elbowing Hunter when he growled under his breath. "Take your time."

"Jesse!" Hunter's exasperated voice echoed behind them as Dagger closed the door.

Jordan chuckled and bowed her head to cover her rosy cheeks. "Well, that was embarrassing," she murmured. "I thought dad was bad. He could take lessons from Hunter."

Dagger chuckled as he opened the door to the transport and helped her onto the seat. "He has a right to be protective. I would be even more so if you were under my care," he said, closing the door and walking around to the other side.

"Where are we going?" Jordan asked in excitement as the transport lifted off the ground.

"I will show you where my home is," he replied. "Then, I will show you some of the areas to the north of the city. It is very beautiful."

"I'd like that," Jordan said, staring at Dagger. "I'd like that very much."

Dagger glanced back at her and smiled. "Hunter has a right to be worried, Jordan," he murmured before focusing on where he was going. "It is just as well you did not greet me in an outfit like your sister did."

"Why?" Jordan asked, unable to stop her curiosity.

"Because if you had…," he replied in a voice that betrayed the heat building inside him. "… the only place you would be seeing today is the inside of my home."

"Oh," she whispered, a slow, satisfied smile curving her lips. "I would like that."

His grunt and muttered curse pulled a bigger grin from her. She folded her hands in her lap, amazed at the scenery far below, but even more amazed that a man like Dagger wanted her. Pleasure burst through her, pouring hope into her young heart.

Perhaps this world would not be so bad after all, she thought, nodding absent-mindedly to the different landmarks that he was pointing out.

* * *

The rest of the afternoon flew by, and much to her chagrin, Dagger was turning the transport toward Jesse and Hunter's home. Jordan sighed as she looked down at the soft glow of lights far below them. Her head turned and she smiled at Dagger when he reached out and cupped her hand in his.

"What is wrong?" He asked, glancing at her.

Jordan shook her head and looked back out of the window. How did she tell him that she didn't want the day to end? That she had never had such a wonderful time and wished it could last forever?

"Nothing," she whispered.

A slight squeeze of her hand told her that he heard the lie in her voice. A soft chuckle escaped when she remembered that Trivators could 'smell' a lie. Releasing a deep breath, she turned to look back at him again.

"I don't want today to end," she said in a quiet voice. "I really enjoyed it, being with you."

Dagger glanced at her face before turning back to look out the front windshield. She reluctantly released his hand when she realized that they were landing. Biting her bottom lip, she wished she had just kept her mouth shut. Tears burned her eyes that he would think she was seeing more into the day than he meant for her to.

The moment the transport landed, she reached for the door. She paused when she felt Dagger's warm hand on her arm. Turning to look at him, she raised her chin.

"Thank you for a wonderful day," she said politely.

"Jordan," Dagger whispered in a husky voice.

Her eyes widened when he reached up and turned her toward him. He stared into her eyes for several long seconds before a low curse escaped him. Her lips parted when he bent his head, meeting him half way.

Pleasure, joy, and relief coursed through her. Her hands slid over his shoulders and her fingers tangled in his hair as she returned his heated kiss with one of her own. She wanted him to know what he was doing to her. She needed him to know that the feelings she felt were not that of a young girl, but of a woman.

Dagger reluctantly pulled back, his eyes flickering over her shoulder at where Hunter stood silhouetted in the front door. His eyes shifted to her with regret. Fear coursed through her at the look of resignation in them.

"Saber and I leave tomorrow morning on a mission," he told her in a grave voice filled with frustration. I am not sure when I will return. I promise when I do, we will not be parted again."

* * *

Jordan jerked back to the present and turned when she felt Dagger's hands sliding down over her shoulders. Brushing a kiss along his jaw, she reached up to undo the fastenings on the shirt he was wearing. When she was finished, she slid her hands back up to push it off his shoulders.

"What were you thinking about?" He asked in a husky voice.

"When you took me for a tour of the mountains not long after we arrived on Rathon," she murmured, tracing the scars on his shoulder with her finger. "Do you remember Saber's reaction to Taylor's outfit?"

A low chuckle escaped Dagger. "Yes, I remember," he replied, bending and pressing his lips to the smooth skin of her shoulder. "The entire day, I kept thinking of what you would look like in such an outfit. I also remember the kiss before I left. I did not sleep well for many nights after that."

"I shouldn't say this, but I'm glad," she moaned when his hands followed her shirt down to her waist and he drew her closer to his body. The feel of her breasts against his hard chest sent a shaft of need through her. "I want you, Dagger. I love you so much."

"Show me," he said.

Jordan pulled back and quickly kicked off her boots and stripped out of the trousers she was wearing. She kicked them to the side, her hands going to still Dagger's when he started to follow her.

"Let me," she whispered. "I want to do this."

Dagger trembled when she slid her hand between the waistband of his trousers and his skin. She smiled as she unfastened them and slowly pulled them down his legs, stopping when they reached his boots. Rising, she gently pushed him back onto the bed. She bent and removed each of his boots before pulling his trousers the rest of the way off and tossing them to the side.

Jordan drew in a sharp breath when she saw just how much he wanted her. Sliding her hands up his thighs, she marveled at the strength she felt in them. Her eyes strayed to a long, thin scar that ran half the length of his left thigh. Bending, she ran her lips along it.

"You are so beautiful," she whispered, meaning it.

He was. He was like Michelangelo's David in the flesh. Her fingers traced the lines, exploring and memorizing him the way he had memorized her. His strength was not only in the flesh, but in the mind as well. To survive the wounds he had received and to continue fighting for as long as he had, told of a man with an inner strength found in few.

She gently cupped his heavy sack, rolling it tenderly between her hands before she moved slightly higher. Each step of her exploration she did first with her hands, second with her eyes, and third with her lips. The muscular body under her stiffened in surprise before a loud hiss exploded from him when she lifted his throbbing cock in her hand and touched her tongue to the tip of it.

Dagger's head jerked down and he stared at her in shock. A soft, husky breath of air danced over the head of it when she chuckled at his wide-eyed amazement. Lowering her head, she kept her eyes locked with his as she took the tip of his cock into her mouth.

"Jordan," he choked out in a husky, rough voice when she pulled back and blew on it.

"Relax," she whispered, teasing the bulbous head with her tongue. "Feel."

* * *

Dagger gave a jerky nod. He didn't know what else to do or say. Hell, he wasn't sure if he could do anything else, much less say anything. What Jordan was doing to him was incredibly erotic and had stunned him to the point he was afraid to say anything that might make her stop.

The females of his species had sharp teeth; teeth made for cutting and tearing. That was not something a warrior wanted wrapped around his cock. Another shudder wracked his body and he wondered if it was possible to go crazy from the pleasure that was coursing through him.

She was stroking his length, up and down, over and over with her sweet lips until he was gripping the sheets and counting backwards in an effort not to explode down her delicate throat. His legs fell apart even farther when she wiggled closer to him.

Dagger laid back and stared up at the ceiling. Watching his cock disappear down her throat, her swollen lips sucking on him... A loud curse shot through him because he knew that he was about to come.

Sitting up, he wrapped his hands around her waist and pulled her up his body. She started to protest, but the look on his face must have given her ample warning that he was at his limit. She opened her legs to him when he aligned her over his cock and slid down over him like a sheath fitting a prized dagger.

"Oh," she hissed as he pushed upward, stretching and filling her.

"Now," he demanded. "Ride me, now."

Jordan cried out when he cupped her breasts and his fingers wrapped around her nipples, pinching the taut peaks until they were rosy and swollen. He demanded she move faster and faster. She rose upward, moving as if she were riding a great beast.

"Come for me, Jordan," he ordered in a hoarse voice. "Come for me."

Jordan threw her head back, clamping down around him and shuddering as her body dissolved around his. He could feel her fisting his cock, pulling his own orgasm from him as her vaginal walls pulsed and squeezed him in a dance that the beast inside him recognized. She was his, in every way, forever.

"I love you, my beautiful warrior," he whispered as she went limp in his arms. "My hope, my Jordan."

Dagger stared up at the ceiling knowing that each and every word he spoke came from his heart. She had captured it as surely as she had rescued him from the cage and chains that had made him a prisoner. She had set him free.

Chapter 18

Jordan gazed around her in delight at the sparkling water early the next morning. She curled her toes in the pink sand and lifted her head to the gentle breeze that teased her with its warm breaths. Shielding her eyes from the glare of the sun off the water, she watched as several fishermen on long flat boards paddled by, cheerfully waving to her. Grinning, she waved back.

They had arrived late last night, and while the planet looked familiar, she couldn't be sure. "That looks just like Rathon," she remembered exclaiming in shock when she saw the planet they were approaching.

"It is. I wanted to spend some time with you, alone," he reluctantly admitted. "Unless you are in a hurry to return to your sisters, if you are, I can change course."

While she had been surprised when he told her that they would not be returning directly to his home, she had been even happier that he wanted to spend time alone with her. The last two weeks they had been on the run or stranded. Either way, both had been filled with the stress of danger.

"No, I'm not ready to go back yet," she replied. "I would love for it to just be the two of us. It will be nice."

Dagger's relieved expression spoke a thousand words to Jordan. He needed time to deal with everything that had happened. While there was no certainty that Kelman was dead, the fact that he was on the run and it was only a matter of time before he was found and prosecuted helped heal the wounds a little. Still, after two years of being caged and fighting to survive, Dagger needed time to adjust to being free. Personally, Jordan was amazed that he was doing as well as he was.

"So, where are we going?" She asked in curiosity.

"There is an island off the coast," he said. "It belongs to a friend of mine. It isn't very populated. There is a small village, but that is all."

"It sounds lovely," Jordan replied. "I think it will be good for the both of us to enjoy some island time, *Mon*."

Dagger's chuckle had filled the bridge at her exaggerated accent. "I like that," he admitted. "Maybe you can wear that outfit you were talking about."

"Maybe I could wear even less," she had countered.

Now, gazing out at the sparkling water, she was glad that he had decided to come here instead of going straight home. While she loved her sisters, Hunter, and his parents, she also knew that she and Dagger needed time together.

"I was wondering where you had disappeared to," Dagger said, walking down onto the beach to stand next to her.

"You were talking to Hunter," she laughed. "Well, arguing would be more like it. I thought it better to leave the two of you alone to work it out. Plus, I couldn't wait any longer. I *had* to know if the sand felt as warm as it looked."

Dagger wrapped his arm around her waist and pulled her closer to his body. "And does it?" He asked in a husky voice. "Feel warmer?"

Jordan turned to him and raised her arms up to his shoulders. He wasn't wearing a shirt and his skin felt just as warm as the sand under her feet. A cloud of memory flashed through her mind for a moment before disappearing.

"What is it?" He asked. "You remembered something."

Jordan rose on her toes and pressed a kiss to his lips. Her fingers wrapped around a strand of hair that curled near his ear. It was growing out.

"I was remembering when we first met," she whispered. "I didn't think I would ever feel warm again, but in your arms..." She paused and drew in a deep breath. "In your arms, I know that I'll never feel the cold."

Dagger pulled her close, holding her as the sun caressed their skin. He knew what she meant now. There had been many days when he wanted to give up. The endless days when the cold of the metal wrapped around his arms and ankles slipped through to his soul. The months of unbearable fatigue from night after night of fighting that had chilled his blood until he shivered uncontrollably under the thin blanket that had been given to him.

"I want to show you something," he murmured.

Jordan took a step back, pushing a strand of long brown hair back behind her ear and smiled. "What?" She asked curiously.

"You'll see," he said with a small smile. "Come."

Jordan tucked her hand in his and followed him back up the narrow path to the terrace of the house built into the rock face. Dagger picked up a colorful blanket and a basket before pulling on her hand again. Laughing, she followed him as he walked up a winding path behind the villa.

"Axe told me about this place years ago," Dagger explained as they walked along the narrow path. "The island has been in his family for centuries. At one time, it was a fortress for a Trivator Prince. His job was to protect the surrounding shoreline."

Jordan reached up and touched a thick, black leaf as they passed under it. Brilliant lines of green light lit up the leaf in delicate patterns. She grinned at Dagger when he turned to look at her.

"This is like the plant on the ship," she laughed. "I knew that I loved you then."

Dagger paused and looked into her eyes. "I knew that you were mine the first time I saw you," he replied. "It is said that at Trivator warrior would know when he had found his *Amate*. It is true. When I saw you lying near the fire… I knew."

Jordan stepped up and wound her arms around his neck, kissing him deeply. He wrapped his free arm around her waist and lifted her up, pressing small kisses along her jaw and lips before running his nose along her cheek. She smelled slightly different, sweeter, than he remembered.

With a groan, he reluctantly set her back on her feet. "If we don't stop, we'll never make it to where I want to take you," he muttered, grabbing her hand and turning her. "It isn't much farther."

Jordan's lips tingled from their kiss. She had never thought of herself as being wanton before, but now all she could do was think of Dagger, usually without his clothes on. He must have sensed her impatience because she felt him squeeze her fingers.

He slowed as the dense coverage of trees and flowering plants thinned. Stepping into a small clearing, she gasped. It was the waterfall from the ship, only this time, it was real. Thick yellow ferns covered the ground like grass. The waterfall sent a prism of color streaming out as the light from the sun caught the mist from it.

Jordan felt tears burning her eyes as she stepped out from under the canopy. She walked over to the crystal clear pool of water and stared down into it. She saw her reflection. The water shimmered and rippled, but she could make out her father's hazel eyes that she had inherited and her mother's small nose and full lips.

She had a scattering of freckles across her nose from playing outside in the sun and had never quite lost them after that. She wasn't beautiful, like Dagger said. Raising her hand, she smoothed back her hair when it blew in front of her face. When she looked again, Dagger was standing beside her, gazing down at their images.

"So much has happened, to both of us," she reflected quietly. "When I look at my reflection, I still see my mom and dad. It gives me strength, knowing that they are still with me, in my heart, a part of who I am."

"What do you see when you look at me, Jordan?" Dagger asked in a somber voice. "Do you see the scars of a warrior? Do you see the heart of a killer?"

Jordan smiled and tears blurred her vision for a brief moment. "I see a man, a warrior, who came out of the darkness and carried me away from the cold. I see a man who warms my heart and makes me feel safe." She turned and took a step closer to him. Raising a hand to his right cheek, she ran her fingers tenderly along the scar. "I see a man who I would follow to the ends of the universe because he makes me feel complete. I see you, Dagger, and I have never seen anything more beautiful in my life."

Tears glistened in Dagger's eyes as he stared down at Jordan. The beast that feared to trust, that fought to survive, calmed inside him as his mate, his *Amate*, touched him with the warmth of her love and healed his battered soul. His throat worked up and down before he closed his eyes and pulled her into his embrace, holding her like he would never let her go, and he wouldn't. She was the reason he had lived. She was his hope.

Pulling back, he held her hand as they walked back to where he had set the blanket and the basket of food he had brought. Together they spread the blanket out under the shade of the tree. Once it was done, he bent and removed a device from the basket. He knelt with her on the blanket, holding the cylinder reverently in his hands.

"This is inscribed with the symbols of my people," he said in a quiet voice. "I am asking you to be my *Amate*, my wife. I have already received permission from Hunter and his and Jesse's acceptance of my claim. I now ask you, Jordan, if you would do me the honor of being my *Amate*."

"Yes, Dagger," Jordan whispered. "Oh, yes."

Dagger swallowed and slipped the device around her right wrist. He snapped it closed and pressed a series of buttons. Drawing in a deep breath, he lifted her left hand to his lips and pressed a soft kiss to her fingers before he guided them to the cylinder.

"Press this," he instructed, watching her. The moment she did, he began to speak in a low, soft voice. "I am Dagger. I belong to Jordan as she belongs to me. Forever will I tie my life to hers. I will care for, protect and give my seed only to her. She is my *Amate*. She is my life. I will protect her and keep her warm, and if the Goddess sees fit, I will give this protection to our children. I love you, Jordan Sampson. Forever."

Jordan knew she was crying, but she was laughing too. He repeated the same ritual when he did her left wrist as well. She swallowed when he showed her how to program the inscription for his wrists.

She carefully snapped the cylinder around his wrist, noting the slight bead of sweat that formed. Raising his left hand to her lips, she kissed the back of his fingers before lowering it to the device. A shudder went through him as the memories of being chained were replaced with the knowledge that this was different.

She held his left hand against her heart after he pressed the command. "I am Jordan. I belong to Dagger as he belongs to me. Forever will I tie my life to his. I will care for, protect and cherish him as he cherishes me. He is my *Amate*. He is my warrior and I love him very, very much."

She carefully removed the cylinder and placed it on his left wrist. This time, the fear, the memory was gone. The only thing she saw was love and warmth.

"I love you, Dagger," she whispered, gazing up at him. "Forever."

"Forever, my *Amate*," he whispered, removing the device when it was finished and tossing it to the side. "My beautiful, little warrior."

Shifting, he slowly removed her clothing, taking his time to explore her in the brilliant light of the sun. Her hair fanned out around her as she lay back against the blanket. His eyes swept over the dark markings wrapped around her pale wrists. His… she was his.

Chapter 19

Dagger grunted and muttered under his breath as he watched Jordan being led away by her sisters. He had barely set the transport he had borrowed down before Taylor had opened the door and pulled Jordan out of it and into her arms. He grimaced when he heard Hunter chuckle.

"What do you think is so funny?" Dagger snapped before he released a sigh. "I did not expect this to be so difficult."

"What? Having an *Amate*?" Hunter asked, slapping Dagger on the shoulder before he pulled him into a bear hug. "I am glad you made it, my friend. I… I apologize for not finding you sooner."

"No, sharing her," Dagger commented as he pulled back. "I understand why you didn't look. You and Saber were injured as well. There was no way of knowing, anyway. I read the reports. I would have thought Edge and I were dead, too. Has there been any word about him?"

Hunter nodded. "Yes, I've sent Thunder and his team to follow up," he replied. "I will not rest until we find either him or his body."

Dagger drew in a deep breath when he saw Saber standing next to the door. A wry smile curved his lips and he strode forward. His eyes hadn't missed the cane his friend was leaning on or the dark shadows in Saber's eyes as Taylor walked by him.

"Saber," Dagger grinned with a nod. "Still as ugly as ever, I see."

Saber's eyes ran over the scar on Dagger's face before he gave him a rueful grin. "They still haven't figured out a way to kill you, have they?" Saber responded.

Dagger nodded to the cane. "I'm not the only one," he replied. "We may not look as good as we did in the past, but that doesn't mean we can't still kill the bastards when we need to."

Saber's mouth tightened when he saw the markings around Dagger's wrists. "Not so much killing anymore," Saber said, turning stiffly and walking into the house.

Hunter frowned as he stared after his friend. The incident last night had nearly pushed Saber over the limit. Taylor was growing up and she let Saber know it, in front of everyone, last night when she ran her hand down the front of his pants and squeezed him. Hunter imagined it was only the shock of what she had done that let her escape from the house, especially when Saber knew that Taylor was meeting a young warrior that was in one of her classes.

"He seems moody," Dagger commented, watching Saber awkwardly walk into the house. "He's lucky to be alive from what I read. You, too, from the incident reports and medical that was in the file."

"Remind me to have a talk with Jordan about hacking into my account," Hunter muttered before he grinned. "Welcome home, Dagger."

Dagger winced when he heard Saber's loud snarl, followed by Taylor's smothered scream. "It's good to be back," he chuckled. "I'm surprised they haven't killed each other yet."

"Taylor is determined that Saber is going to get off his 'ass' as she puts it and 'get back to the living'," Hunter remarked with a grin. "She is slowly succeeding. He comes over almost every day with one excuse or another. I think he is realizing that if he doesn't, he just might lose the best thing that ever happened to him."

Both men stepped to one side when Taylor stormed by them, her face a mask of fury. Saber wasn't far behind her. It was the fastest that Hunter had seen his friend move in the past two years.

"You aren't the boss of me," Taylor yelled over her shoulder. "I can hang with whoever I want, you big lout. I'm a woman! I turned eighteen months ago if you hadn't noticed!"

"I forbid you to go anywhere near that boy again," Saber yelled, pushing past them.

"Bite me," Taylor called out, slamming the gate. "Hunter, I'll be back in a few."

Dagger watched as Taylor took off running. Her hair swung behind her and she ran with long, confident strides. She had grown up over the past two years.

"Is she always like that?" Dagger asked, thinking of how different, and yet how similar, she was to Jordan.

"Only when Saber is near," Hunter replied with a sigh. "Let's go in the house. He'll wait on the porch until she comes back. He always does."

Dagger nodded. Saber stood at the gate, staring down the long path. He was leaning heavily on the cane, but at least he was moving. Turning, he smiled when he saw Shana and Scout.

Yes, it is good to be home, he thought with a grin.

* * *

It was well after midnight before they finally made it to his house. Dagger set the transport down inside the circled courtyard after disabling the protective barrier. It felt strange being back. While he had owned this house for years, it had never really felt like a home. It had just been a place to sleep between missions.

Now, it would be different. Jordan would be here and he would no longer go on missions. He decided he had enough of that life. Instead, he would focus on training the young warriors coming up, including his own sons one day.

Dagger slid from the seat of the transport and walked around to help Jordan down. He jerked in surprise when he felt a sudden sting in his left shoulder. Reaching up, he felt the back of his shirt.

His fingers wrapped around the long, thin cylinder and he jerked on it. Looking down at it, he swayed as his body grew heavy. The dart fell from his fingers and he rolled to the side of the transport.

"Dagger," Jordan's husky voice cried out as she knelt beside him.

Dagger blinked and tried to clear his vision as a shadowy figure stepped out of the dark. He tried to rise when he saw the second figure that stepped out.

His mouth tightened and he braced his hand on the ground, but couldn't get his legs to cooperate.

"Run," he forced out, shifting his eyes to Jordan. "Run."

Jordan turned when she heard the sound of muted clapping. She hissed and tried to move in front of Dagger. Her hands clenched as she stared into the dark, cold eyes of Cordus Kelman.

"No!" She growled in rage, slowly rising to her feet. "I *will not* let you harm him again."

Kelman chuckled in amusement. "You have fire in you for someone so small," he laughed. "I'll give you a choice, come with me quietly and I'll let him live. If you refuse, I kill him now. He has cost me a significant amount of my resources and wealth. I expect for him to help replenish it."

"You heartless bastard," Jordan hissed, stepping in front of Dagger. "Those are living beings you put in those cages. Their lives are worth more than a few credits! They have families that care about them, love them, and you… you rip that away."

"What planet are you from?" Kelman asked, shaking his head in wonder. "It would be interesting watching them in a fight ring. I can't believe you have continued to exist."

Jordan straightened up and her eyes grew cold and hard. "You know nothing of my species," she replied in a calm voice devoid of emotion. "You wouldn't survive a day on my world."

Kelman released a long, deep breath. "Cuff her," he ordered the dark figure standing silently beside him.

The figure moved forward on silent feet. Jordan tried to jerk back, but Kelman pulled a weapon and aimed it a Dagger's unconscious form. Nausea built inside her when the male indicated that she should put her hands out in front of her. Jordan forced herself to remain still as the man slipped the cuffs around each of her wrists and attached them in the center.

"What are you planning to do?" Jordan asked, wishing she thought to grab the laser pistol at Dagger's waist when he fell.

Kelman walked forward and grabbed her by the arm. She stumbled when he pushed her forward, toward the gate. She couldn't help, but glance over to where Dagger laid, leaning sideways on the ground.

"I want him hungry, and willing," Kelman chuckled. "If I put you in the center of the cage, he will fight anything I put in there."

"You know they have places for creatures like you," Jordan retorted, hoping that someone would be out and about at this time of the night. "You are crazy."

Kelman jerked Jordan to a stop at the entrance to the gate and stared down at her through narrowed eyes. A slow smile curved his lips when he saw the fear she was trying to hide. Satisfied that she wouldn't be any trouble, he turned back to the figure following a short distance behind them.

"Shoot him in the legs," Kelman ordered. "I don't want him to follow us too soon."

"No!" Jordan cried, trying to turn back toward Dagger. "No!"

Kelman grabbed her arm and slapped her across the face, before he pressed the end of the laser pistol against her shoulder. Jordan pulled in a shaky breath, but she didn't fight him. She got the message. He would shoot her as well if she didn't follow his instructions. All he needed was for her to be alive.

"I hope he kills you," she whispered in a trembling breath.

"You and a million others out there," Kelman chuckled, even as he roughly turned her around and pushed her through the gate. "I just make sure that I kill them first."

* * *

Dagger fought against the drug coursing through his system. His partially numb fingers moved down to his waist and fumbled for the laser pistol he was wearing. He was lying on his side, tilted forward, so neither Kelman nor the assassin he had hired saw the movement of his hand under his jacket.

Kelman had finally made a deadly mistake. Over the past two years, Dagger had been pumped full of the sedatives so many times, that his body had developed a resistance to it until it took a larger dose to knock him out. The small dose might have knocked him down, but it hadn't totally incapacitated him.

Dagger heard what Kelman planned to do. This time, he was going to finish the man. His fingers tightened around the grip of the laser pistol when he heard Kelman order the man to shoot him.

Breathing deeply, he counted the number of steps as they approached, trying to judge the distance from the man. Cracking his eyelids, he waited until he saw the tips of the black boots before he rolled slightly and fired two shots into the male. He hit him once in the chest and the second time between the eyes.

He forced his sluggish muscles to move as he pulled himself over to the assassin. One thing he had learned during his years at war, was if you were going to use a drug on someone, you'd better carry an antidote in case it got used on you. He rolled over onto his back, focusing on moving his right arm and hand.

Patting the man's jacket, he moved down to the weapons belt. His fingers slid over a small pouch. Sweat glistened on his forehead as he fumbled for what seemed like endless minutes, but in reality was probably only a few seconds, to open it. He slid his fingers in, and grabbed the small injector.

Rolling onto his side, he pulled the injector toward his mouth and pulled the cap off of it. Forcing his hand down, he pressed it against his leg and depressed the trigger. Almost immediately, he could feel the paralysis holding his muscles in their greedy grasp release. It took almost a full minute before he felt like he was back in control of his body.

Rolling stiffly to his feet, he strode over to the transport. He jerked the comlink that was lying in the center console out, and attached it to his ear at the same time as he reached for the black bag behind the seats. Ripping it open, he began pulling out the weapons he would need.

"Speak," a deep voice growled in his ear.

"Kelman has Jordan," Dagger replied.

There was a fraction of silence before he heard Hunter's voice again. "How? Where?"

"My house. Now," Dagger answered. "He has to have a ship waiting. Find it and take it out."

"Done," Hunter replied. "I'm on my way."

"He was on foot," Dagger warned him. "He must have a transport hidden."

"He'll have to stay on the path," Hunter answered him. "I'll be there in less than ten."

Dagger shut off the comlink. He would know when Hunter arrived. Clipping the belt around his waist, he palmed the pistol in his hand and took off. The beast inside him had awoken. This time, there would be no denying him his kill.

Chapter 20

Jordan fought the urge to cry. The faint sounds of laser fire had echoed through the night. She couldn't keep the choked sob from escaping at the knowledge of what had just happened to Dagger.

"I hate you," she hissed, stumbling along the dark path.

Kelman released an irritated sigh. "I thought you might be a touch more original than the others," he drawled impatiently, glancing behind him in frustration. The assassin should have caught up with them. "Move."

Jordan stumbled again on the uneven path when he shoved her between her shoulder blades. Fury built inside her, boiling over. Memories, both past and present, poured through her mind. Images flashed through her in vivid detail of all the years she, Jesse, and Taylor had spent running and the hiding. She remembered the day the Trivators came and her dad died. She remembered the years she and her sisters had spent fighting for a scrap of food or a decent night's sleep or just trying to live.

"No," she hissed, slowly turning to face him.

Kelman glared at her in surprise. "What did you just say?" He asked in disbelief.

Jordan took a step toward him. Beside her, she heard the sound of a branch cracking. Déjà vu swept through her as she remembered the night just a few months ago when she was walking along a path similar to this one. Grim determination filled her as she stepped up to Kelman and pushed him – *hard* - in the chest.

"I… said… No!" Jordan growled. "I won't move. I won't go with you. I won't let you hurt Dagger any more than you already have. I… Won't… Let… You!"

Shock crossed Kelman's face before it darkened with irritation. Jordan saw him raise his hand to strike her across the face again. This time, she was ready for it. Reaching up, she grabbed his arm and twisted around like her dad had taught her and let the forward momentum of his body carry him over her shoulder.

She stood up, staring down at Kelman's body in shock for a brief second before she realized that he had dropped the pistol he was holding. She moved quickly and kicked it off the path and into the grassy section on the other side of the soft, red lights. A low cry escaped her when Kelman rolled and grabbed her by the ankle.

She fell and rolled, kicking at him when he tried to pull her toward him. Shuffling backwards, she rolled to her feet and tried to run. Kelman had risen as well and wrapped an arm around her waist. Jordan reacted violently, swinging around with her elbow into his cheekbone at the same time as she twisted away from him.

The move knocked him backwards several steps toward the edge of the path. Jordan had lost her balance again as she turned and fell hard on her right hip. She immediately rolled, pushing herself up into a crouching position as Kelman wiped at the blood from where she had broken the skin along his cheek.

"I am going to enjoy torturing you," he snarled. "I'll make sure your Trivator gets to watch while I do it."

Jordan swallowed when she saw the glow of red eyes in the woods behind Kelman. Her eyes flickered to him, then to the pistol lying just outside of the path. Kelman glanced down and behind him. A slow smile curved his lips as he took a step back. He was still on the path, but it wouldn't take much to push him off. If she could…

Jordan didn't think. Darting forward, she raised her hands and caught Kelman in the center of his chest with her hands, shoving him backwards off the protected path. She stumbled to a stop when he fell backwards onto the soft ground.

Her eyes widened when he slowly stood up, picking up the laser pistol as he did. She started to take a step backwards when he shook his head and aimed it at her. Jordan's heart pounded as he took a step closer to the path. She couldn't see the glow of red eyes any longer. Had the creature been frightened off? Had it been just a figment of her wishful imagination? Raising her hands out in front of her, she drew in a deep breath.

"Please," she whispered. "I can't lose him. I… can't…"

"Ask me if I care," Kelman replied with a mocking sneer.

"I do," a deep voice replied right before a flare of light lit the night.

* * *

Dagger fired the laser pistol, hitting Kelman in the shoulder and knocking him to the side. He had come up on them just as Jordan had turned on the man. He was still too far away to fire, especially with them fighting, but he had heard every defiant word she had spoken to the cold mercenary.

He had been shocked when he saw her fighting back. When she had thrown Kelman over her shoulder, he almost shouted out. Instead, he had come forward with the intention of saving her. It took a moment for him to realize what she was doing when she had knocked Kelman off the path. Dagger could have sworn he had seen the glowing red eyes of one of the forest predators that came out at night watching what was going on.

"Jordan, are you hurt?" Dagger asked in concern, glancing at where Kelman lay moaning.

"N... No," she whispered in a broken voice. "I heard the shots. Kelman told that man to shoot you. I heard the shots."

"It was me doing the shooting," Dagger murmured. He turned when the sound of running feet echoed in the quietness of the night. "It is Hunter."

"Hunter!" Jordan repeated hoarsely as shock began to set in and she began to shake. "I don't..."

Jordan cried out when an arm grabbed her and tried to pull her toward him. Kelman's fingers dug painfully into her arm. She stared at his pale face. Blood dripped from the corner of his mouth and a gurgling sound escaped his throat as his mouth was opening and closing.

Jordan heard the loud sound of a woman's scream, the sound high and piercing. She knew the sound was coming from her, but her eyes were glued to the creature attached to the other end of Kelman. The huge, six-legged creature was pulling Kelman toward the woods. Her eyes moved down to where Kelman's fingers gripped her arm in a death grip, pulling her with him.

"Jordan!" Dagger cried out in horror. "Pull his fingers free of her arm. Cut his arm off if you have to!" Dagger shouted to Hunter.

Hunter grimly pulled Kelman's fingers free of her arm. The moment she was free, she collapsed into a shaking mass in Dagger's arms. Her eyes were wide, her mouth open, but the screaming had stopped. No sound escaped her, except the sounds of her loud panting.

"It's okay," he whispered, using the words he had learned back on Earth to soothe her. "Everything will be alright. He's gone. He's gone."

Jordan's eyelashes fluttered as she looked up at Hunter. He was standing over Dagger's shoulder, looking down at her with concern. Her eyes shifted to Dagger and she locked her eyes with him as her teeth began to chatter.

"Co...Cold," she whispered. "Pl... Please... Cold... Warm me."

"Always," Dagger whispered, pulling her closer to him as her eyes closed against her pale cheeks. "I'll always keep you warm."

"Saber has arrived with the transport," Hunter said in a quiet voice. "Let's get her to medical."

Dagger looked up at Hunter and nodded. Rising, he refused to release Jordan. Her body was so light, so delicate, so fragile, yet she was the strongest woman he had ever known.

No! I won't move. I won't go with you. I won't let you hurt Dagger any more than you already have. I... Won't... Let... You!

And she hadn't he thought as he carried her over to where Saber was waiting with the transport. He slid into the seat. Hunter climbed into the front. A soft murmur had Saber lifting off the ground.

Dagger stared blindly out at the night as they rose into the air. His arms tightened around Jordan's slender figure. It was over. Kelman was dead. Bowing his head, he closed his eyes and pressed a kiss to the top of Jordan's head. He was free.

* * *

Jordan's face turned to the sun as a sliver of it shone across her face. She blinked, immediately recognizing where she was. A smile curved her lips when a light breeze blew the sheer curtains open to reveal the tops of the tropical trees. In the distance, she could hear the sound of the waves on the beach and the 'birds' that populated this world.

Turning her head, the smile on her face softened and grew tender when she locked gazes with

Dagger's warm yellow-gold eyes. She closed her eyes when he reached up and traced the curve of her cheek. Turning her head, she pressed a kiss to the center of his palm.

"Good morning," she whispered.

"Good morning," Dagger replied in the rough, husky voice that she loved so much. "How are you feeling?"

Jordan frowned, concentrating as she did a mental evaluation of her body. She felt… good. The frown turned to relief when she thought of what had happened back on the mainland.

"Is it true?" She asked, opening her eyes and looking at him. "He's gone, for good?"

Dagger rolled onto his side and cupped a hand under his head. He played with the silky strands of her hair for a moment before he ran his finger down along her jaw. He would never get tired of touching her.

"Yes, Kelman's gone for good," he replied.

Jordan rolled onto her side so that she was facing him. Reaching up, she stroked the scar on his cheek before rubbing her thumb along his bottom lip. She smiled when he nipped at it.

"How long was I asleep?" She asked, staring up into his eyes.

"Too long," he whispered. "Every second you didn't wake, I worried. I love you, Jordan. You make each day a new one for me. I need you."

"You once said I was what gave you hope," she told him. "It works both ways. You took me out of the darkness. You brought light and love and filled my heart. You were my hope, Dagger. I couldn't lose that. I won't. You promised me forever and I want every second of it. If you ever get lost again, I'll find you. I'll come for you, no matter what."

Dagger's eyes closed and he reached up to hold her fingers against his lips. Jordan felt the shudder that went through him before he opened his eyes. He pressed their joined hands against his ravaged cheek and smiled.

"I won't get lost again. I have too much here to ever leave it," he told her in a husky voice. "I'm going to build a home for us here. Our son will grow strong and I'll teach him to be a warrior who will one day be given an *Amate* as beautiful and as brave as his mother. And if we are given the gift of a daughter, then I will protect her and keep her warm just as I promised her mother I would do. I have a family, Jordan. You and our son, are just the beginning of what I had always hoped to have."

"A son," Jordan whispered in shock. "How…? Are you sure?"

Dagger rolled, caging her under his long length. His eyes softened and he bent to press a tender kiss to her lips. Tracing a path down to her ear, he rubbed his nose along her neck.

"I'm very sure, my *Amate*. The healer at the medical centre was concerned and cautioned me to make sure that you were not placed in danger again," Dagger murmured, pressing a kiss to her neck.

"Thank you, Jordan Sampson. Thank you for believing in your heart and finding me."

"Forever," she whispered, losing herself in his love.

To be continued....

Challenging Saber: The Alliance Book 4

If you loved this story by me (S.E. Smith) please leave a review. You can also take a look at additional books and sign up for my newsletter at **http://sesmithfl.com** to hear about my latest releases or keep in touch using the following links:

Website: http://sesmithfl.com
Newsletter: http://sesmithfl.com/?s=newsletter
Facebook: https://www.facebook.com/se.smith.5
Twitter: https://twitter.com/sesmithfl
Pinterest: http://www.pinterest.com/sesmithfl/
Blog: http://sesmithfl.com/blog/
Forum: http://www.sesmithromance.com/forum/

Excerpts of S.E. Smith Books

If you would like to read more S.E. Smith stories, she recommends Touch of Frost, the first in her Magic, New Mexico series. Or if you prefer a Paranormal or Western with a twist, you can check out Lily's Cowboys or Indiana Wild…

Additional Books by S.E. Smith

Short Stories and Novellas
For the Love of Tia
         (Dragon Lords of Valdier Book 4.1)
A Dragonling's Easter
         (Dragonlings of Valdier Book 1.1)
A Dragonling's Haunted Halloween
         (Dragonlings of Valdier Book 1.2)

A Dragonling's Magical Christmas
(Dragonlings of Valdier Book 1.3)
A Warrior's Heart
(Marastin Dow Warriors Book 1.1)
Rescuing Mattie
(Lords of Kassis: Book 3.1)

Science Fiction/Paranormal Novels

Cosmos' Gateway Series

Tink's Neverland (Cosmos' Gateway: Book 1)
Hannah's Warrior (Cosmos' Gateway: Book 2)
Tansy's Titan (Cosmos' Gateway: Book 3)
Cosmos' Promise (Cosmos' Gateway: Book 4)
Merrick's Maiden (Cosmos' Gateway Book 5)

Curizan Warrior

Ha'ven's Song (Curizan Warrior: Book 1)

Dragon Lords of Valdier

Abducting Abby (Dragon Lords of Valdier: Book 1)
Capturing Cara (Dragon Lords of Valdier: Book 2)
Tracking Trisha (Dragon Lords of Valdier: Book 3)
Ambushing Ariel (Dragon Lords of Valdier: Book 4)
Cornering Carmen (Dragon Lords of Valdier: Book 5)
Paul's Pursuit (Dragon Lords of Valdier: Book 6)
Twin Dragons (Dragon Lords of Valdier: Book 7)

Lords of Kassis Series

River's Run (Lords of Kassis: Book 1)
Star's Storm (Lords of Kassis: Book 2)
Jo's Journey (Lords of Kassis: Book 3)
Ristéard's Unwilling Empress (Lords of Kassis: Book 4)

Magic, New Mexico Series

Touch of Frost (Magic, New Mexico Book 1)
Taking on Tory (Magic, New Mexico Book 2)

Sarafin Warriors

Choosing Riley (Sarafin Warriors: Book 1)

Viper's Defiant Mate (Sarafin Warriors Book 2)
The Alliance Series
Hunter's Claim (The Alliance: Book 1)
Razor's Traitorous Heart (The Alliance: Book 2)
Dagger's Hope (The Alliance: Book 3)
Zion Warriors Series
Gracie's Touch (Zion Warriors: Book 1)
Krac's Firebrand (Zion Warriors: Book 2)
Paranormal and Time Travel Novels
Spirit Pass Series
Indiana Wild (Spirit Pass: Book 1)
Spirit Warrior (Spirit Pass Book 2)
Second Chance Series
Lily's Cowboys (Second Chance: Book 1)
Touching Rune (Second Chance: Book 2)
Young Adult Novels
Breaking Free Series
Voyage of the Defiance (Breaking Free: Book 1)

Recommended Reading Order Lists:
http://sesmithfl.com/reading-list-by-events/
http://sesmithfl.com/reading-list-by-series/

About S.E. Smith

S.E. Smith is a *New York Times, USA TODAY, International, and Award-Winning* Bestselling author of science fiction, fantasy, paranormal, and contemporary works for adults, young adults, and children. She enjoys writing a wide variety of genres that pull her readers into worlds that take them away.